FRANKLIN PARK PUBLIC LIBRARY

3 1316 00063 9768

W9-APJ-335

LEGO® BIONICLE

GATHERING OF THE TOA

FRANKLIN PARK PUBLIC LIBRARY
Franklin Park, Illinois

Story by Ryder Windham

Art by Caravan Studio

Ⓛ Ⓑ

Little, Brown and Company
New York • Boston

This book is a work of fiction. Names, characters, places, and incidents are the product of the author's imagination or are used fictitiously. Any resemblance to actual events, locales, or persons, living or dead, is coincidental.

LEGO, the LEGO logo, and BIONICLE are trademarks of the LEGO Group.

Produced by Little, Brown and Company under license from the LEGO Group. © 2015 The LEGO Group

Line art by Faisal P
Colors by Felix H, Kate, Angie, Indra, Ifan, Hazmi, and Rendra

In accordance with the U.S. Copyright Act of 1976, the scanning, uploading, and electronic sharing of any part of this book without the permission of the publisher is unlawful piracy and theft of the author's intellectual property. If you would like to use material from the book (other than for review purposes), prior written permission must be obtained by contacting the publisher at permissions@hbgusa.com. Thank you for your support of the author's rights.

Little, Brown and Company

Hachette Book Group
1290 Avenue of the Americas, New York, NY 10104
Visit us at lb-kids.com

Little, Brown and Company is a division of Hachette Book Group, Inc. The Little, Brown name and logo are trademarks of Hachette Book Group, Inc.

The publisher is not responsible for websites (or their content) that are not owned by the publisher.

First Edition: December 2015

Library of Congress Control Number: 2015952251

Paperback ISBN: 978-0-316-26622-2
Paper over Board ISBN: 978-0-316-30912-7

10 9 8 7 6 5 4 3 2 1

LAKE

Printed in the United States of America

THE PROPHECY

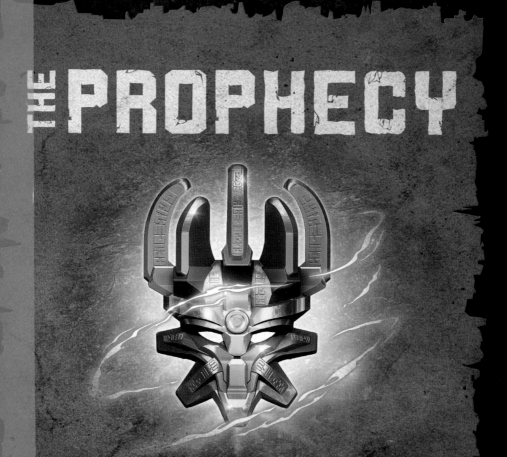

It was pieced together by fragments, whispered to the people of Okoto thousands of years ago when they found the lifeless body of Ekimu the Mask Maker. The prophecy has been told around the campfires as part of the legacy of the Protectors, and handed down through the generations from father to son...

J-G
LEGO BIONICL
63-9768

When times are dark
and all hope seems lost,

The Protectors
must unite,

One from each tribe,

Evoke the power of
past and future

And look to the skies
for an answer.

When the stars align,

Six comets will bring
timeless heroes

To claim the
masks of power

And find the Mask Maker.

United, the elements hold
the power to defeat evil.

United but not one.

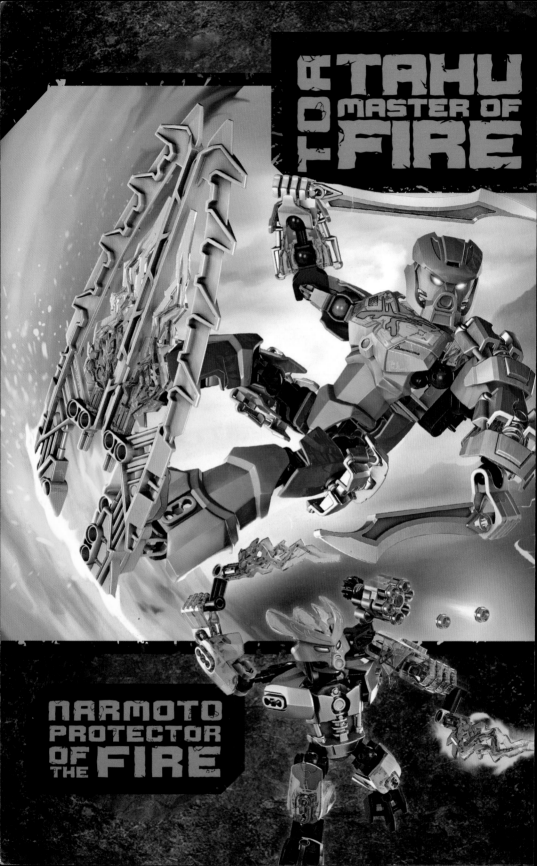

TAHU MASTER OF FIRE

NARMOTO PROTECTOR OF THE FIRE

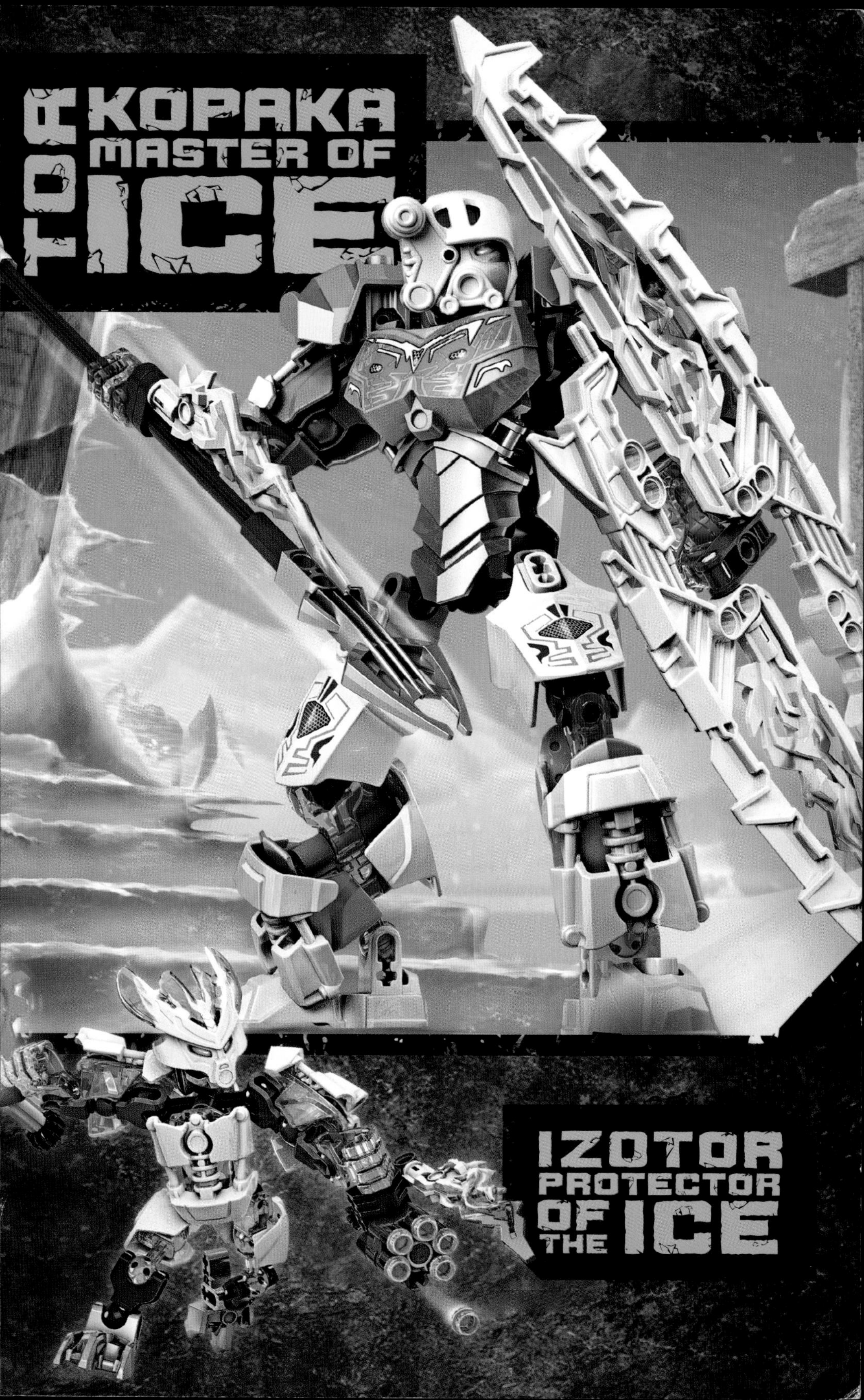
TOA
KOPAKA
MASTER OF
ICE
IZOTOR
PROTECTOR
OF THE ICE

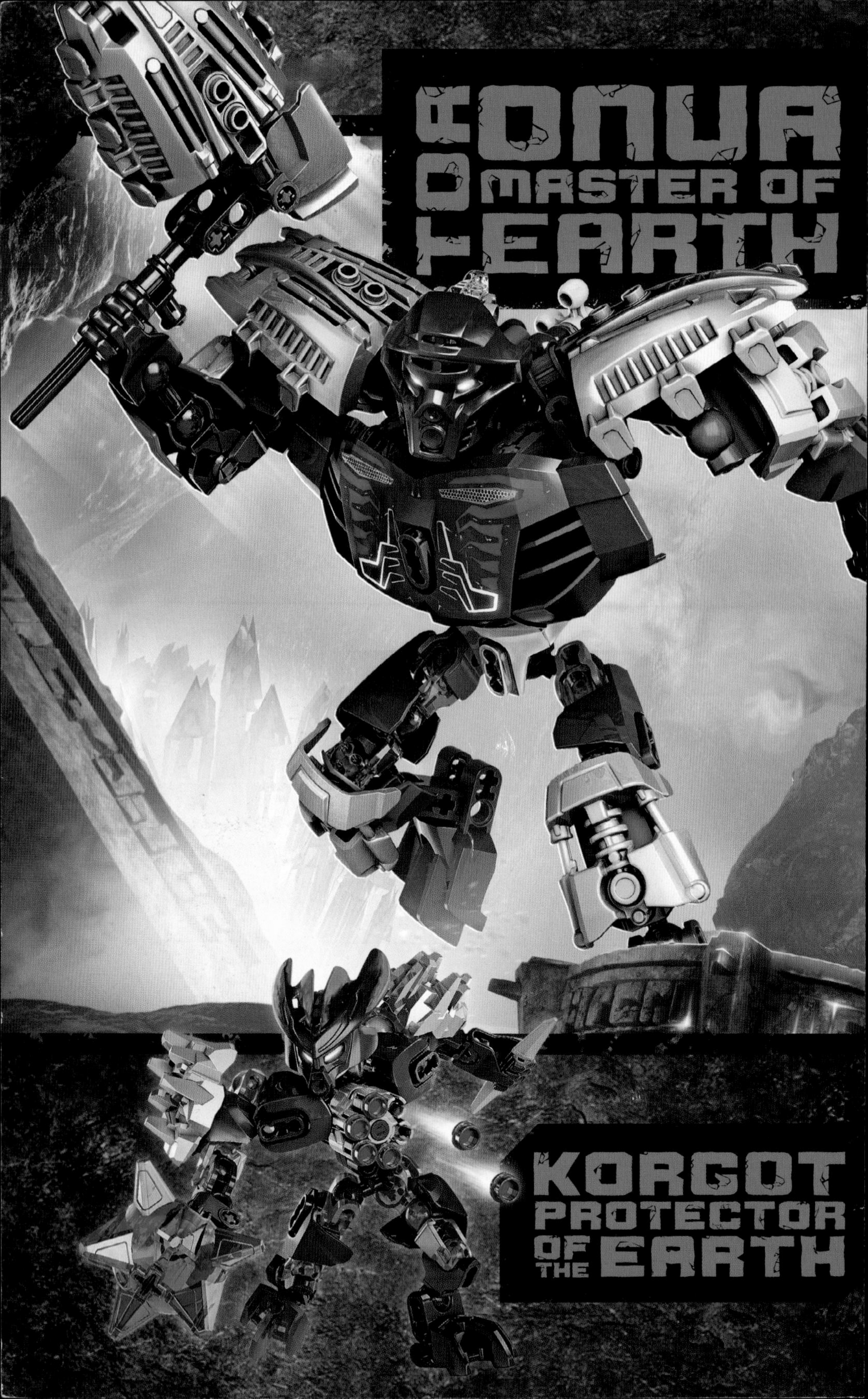
TOA ONUA MASTER OF EARTH
KORGOT PROTECTOR OF THE EARTH

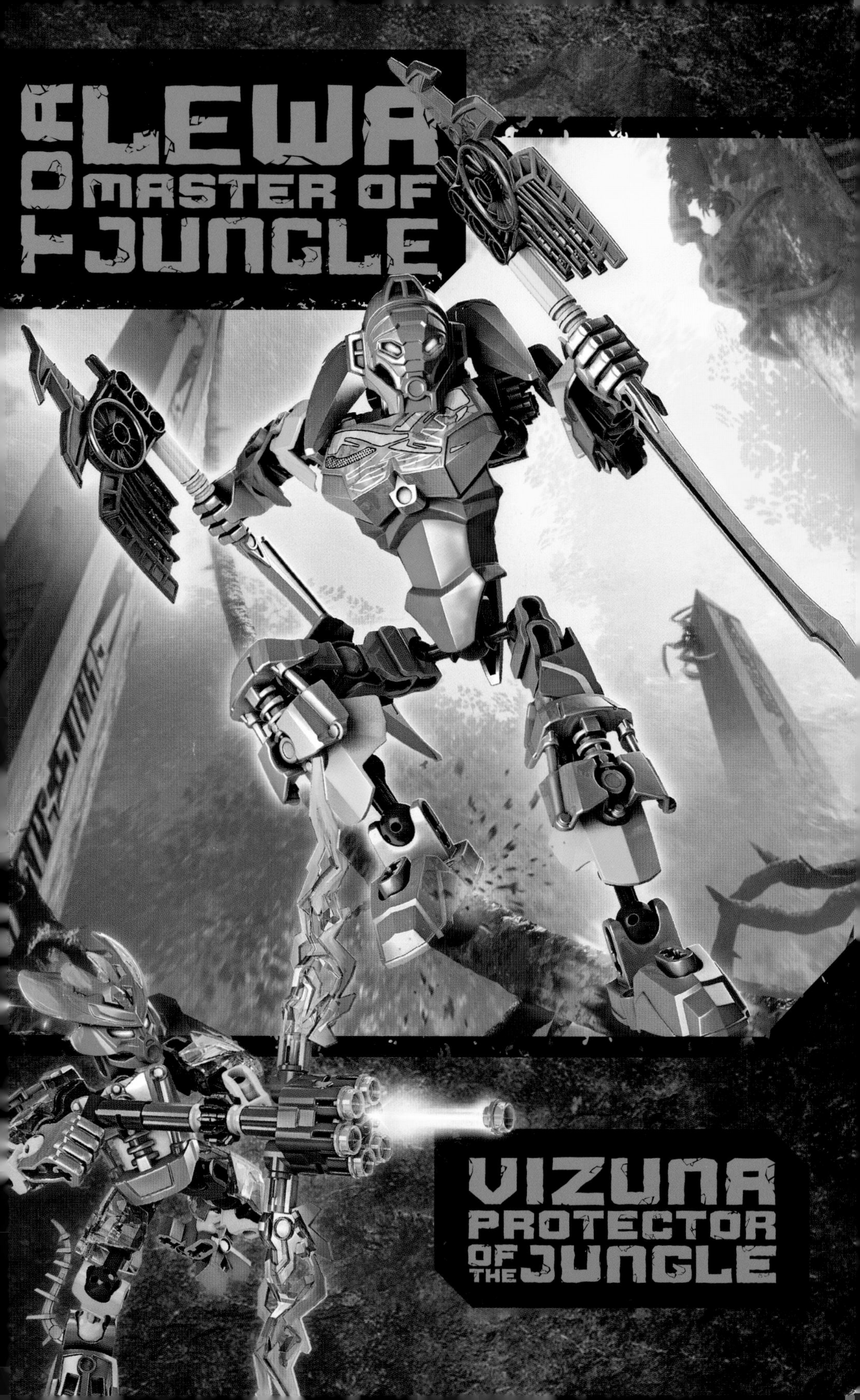
TOA
LEWA
MASTER OF
JUNGLE
VIZUNA
PROTECTOR
OF THE
JUNGLE

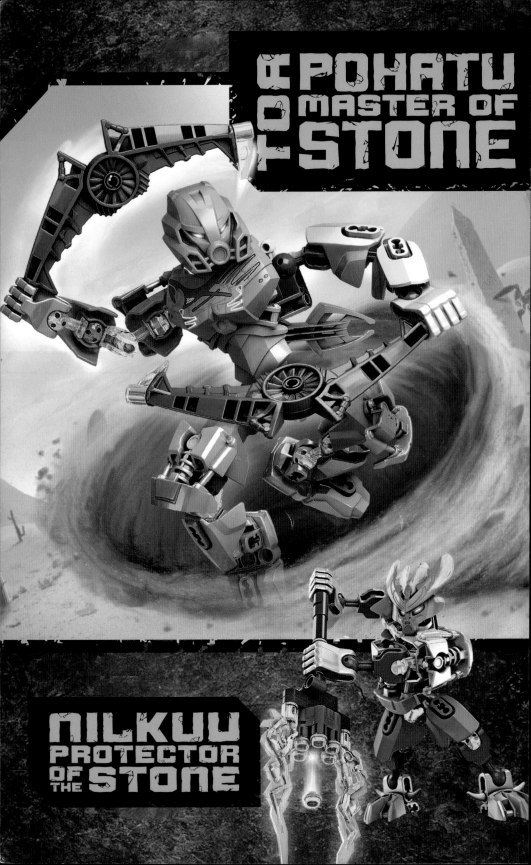

POHATU
MASTER OF STONE

NILKUU
PROTECTOR OF THE STONE

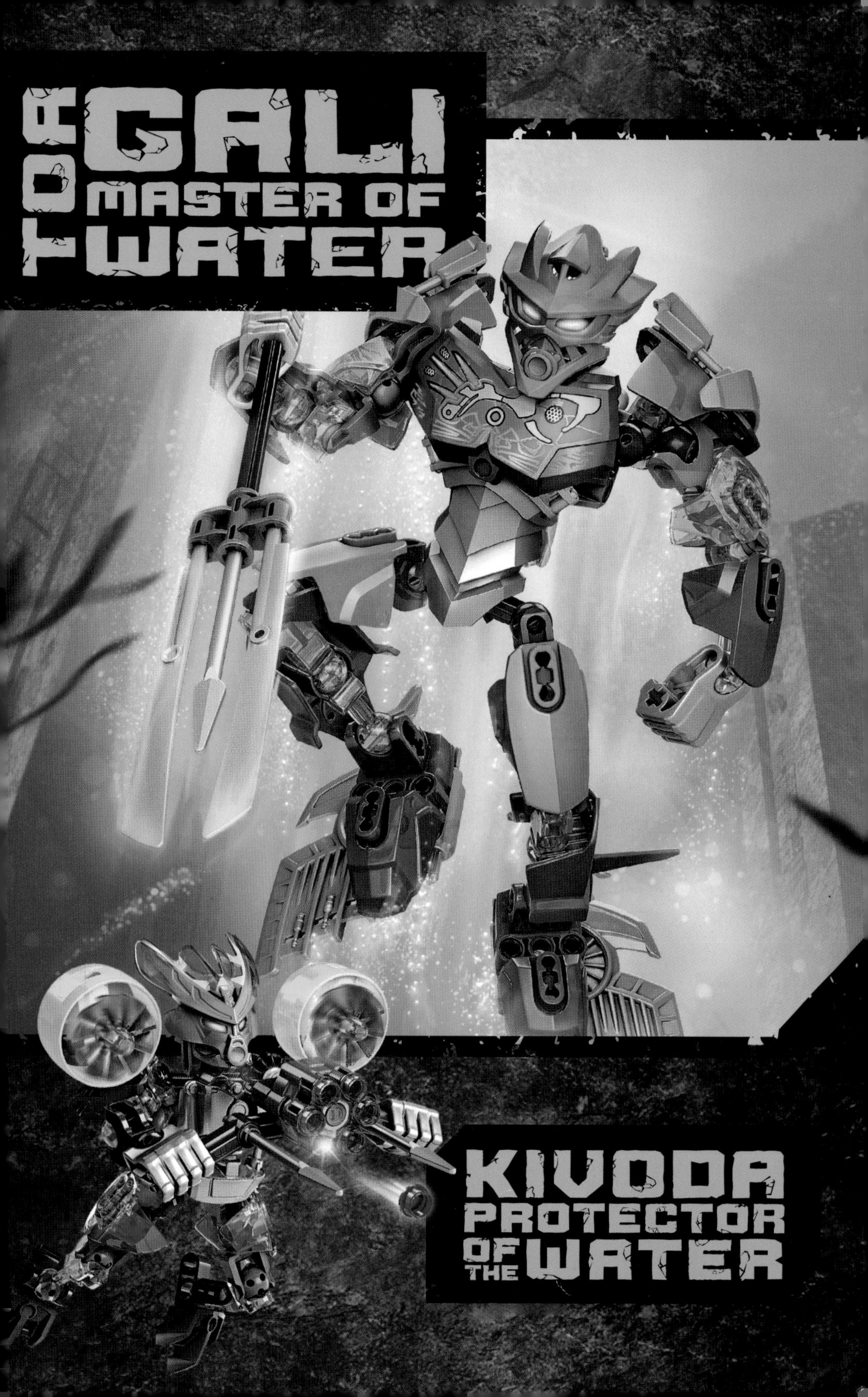
TOA
GALI
MASTER OF
WATER
KIVODA
PROTECTOR
OF THE
WATER

GATHERING OF THE TOA

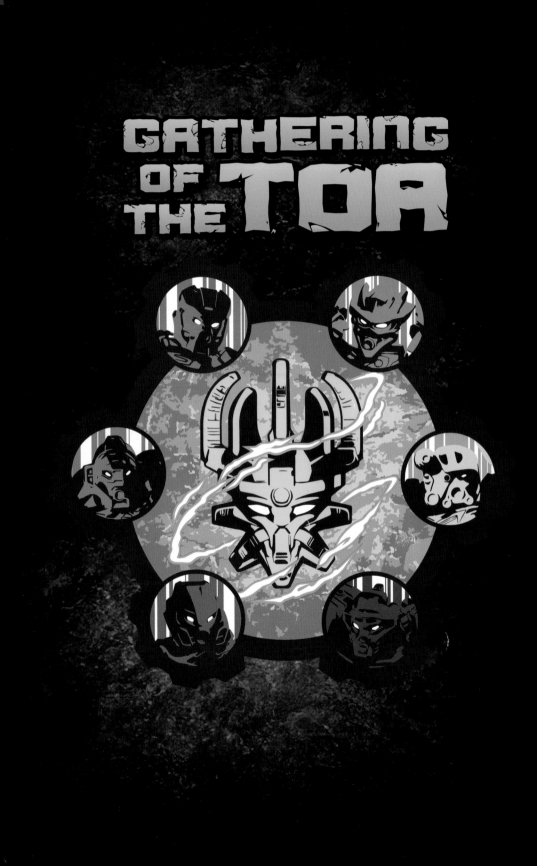

THE PROTECTORS IN *HELP FROM BEYOND*

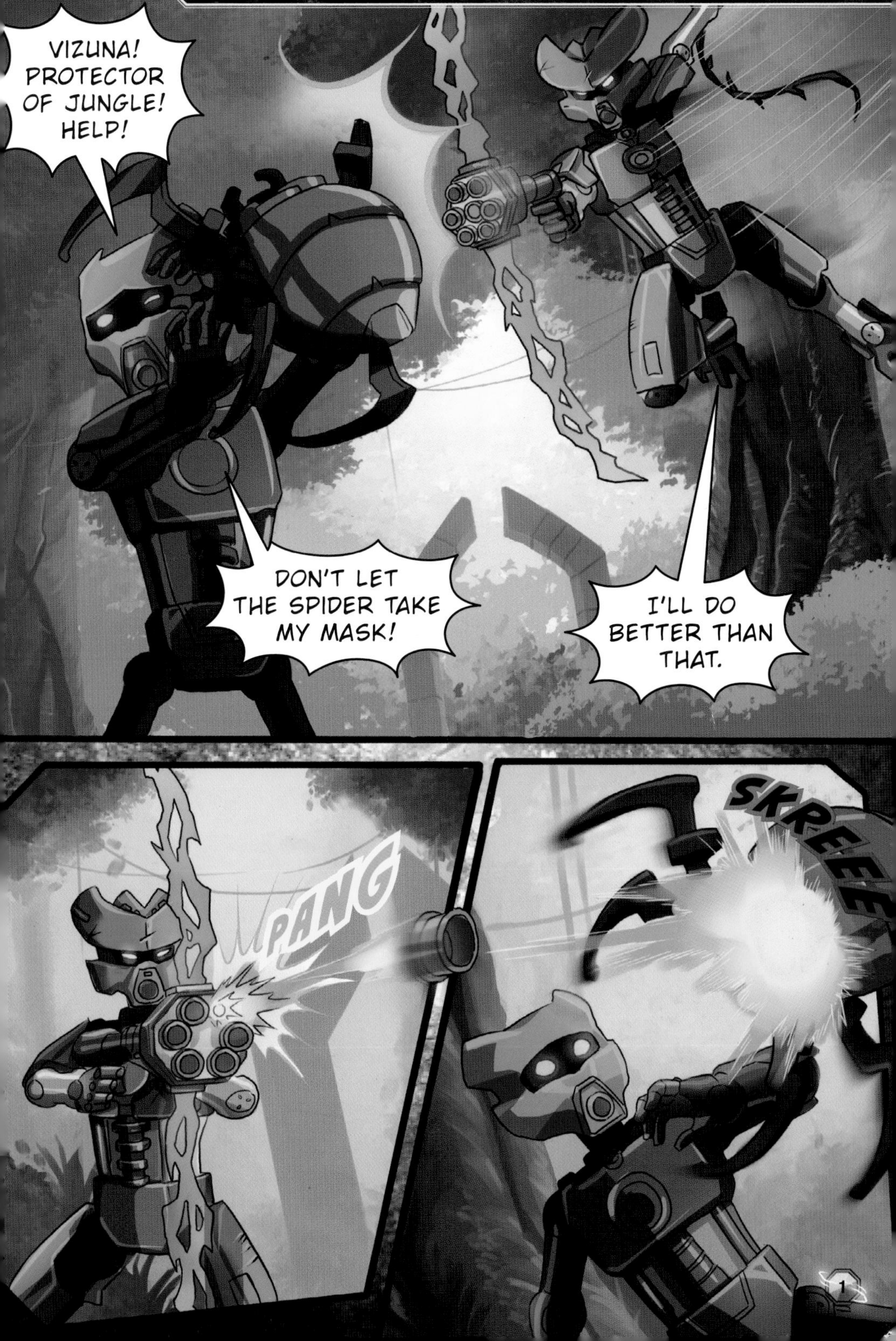
VIZUNA! PROTECTOR OF JUNGLE! HELP!
DON'T LET THE SPIDER TAKE MY MASK!
I'LL DO BETTER THAN THAT.
PANG
SKREEEE

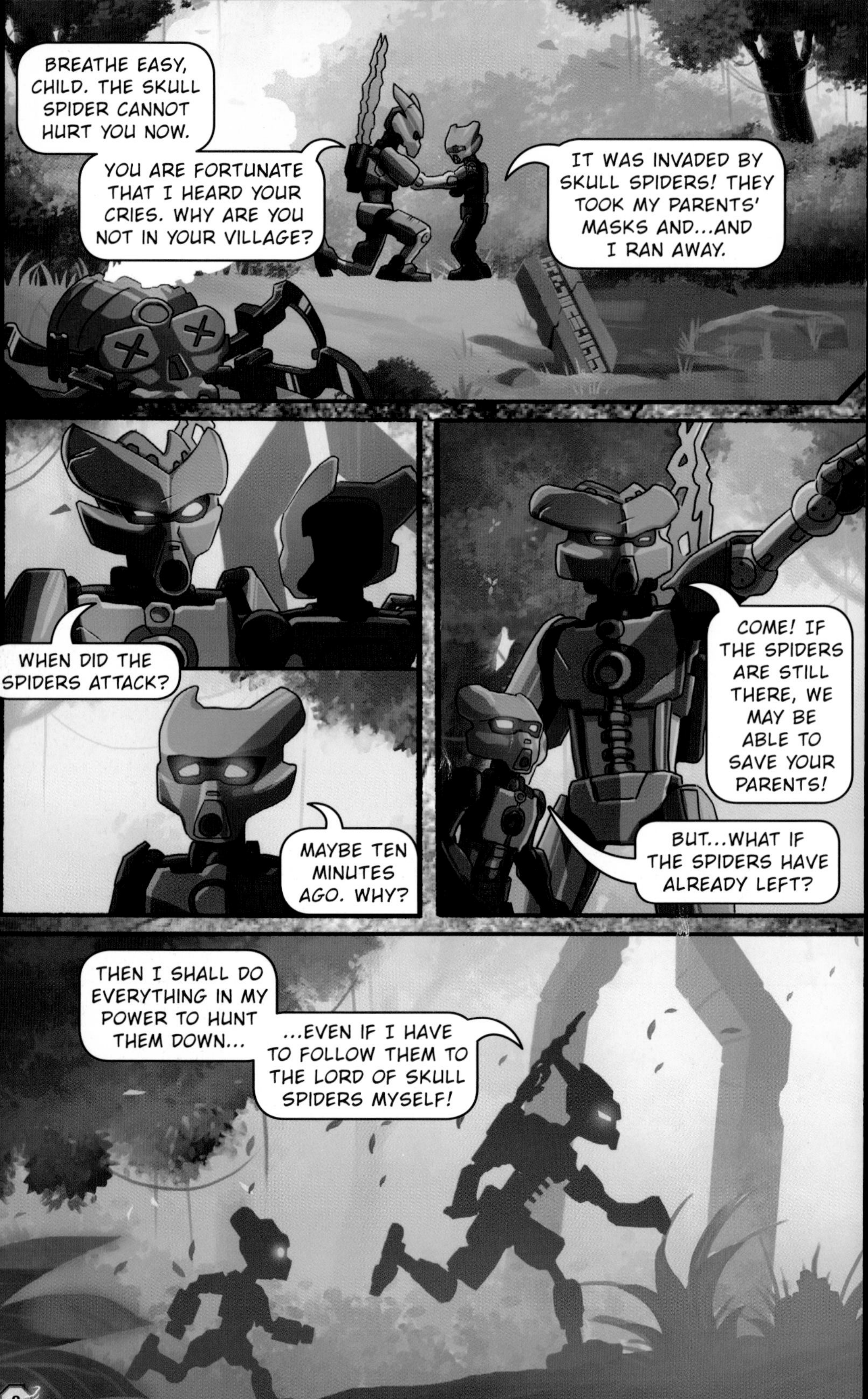
BREATHE EASY, CHILD. THE SKULL SPIDER CANNOT HURT YOU NOW.
YOU ARE FORTUNATE THAT I HEARD YOUR CRIES. WHY ARE YOU NOT IN YOUR VILLAGE?
IT WAS INVADED BY SKULL SPIDERS! THEY TOOK MY PARENTS' MASKS AND...AND I RAN AWAY.
WHEN DID THE SPIDERS ATTACK?
MAYBE TEN MINUTES AGO. WHY?
COME! IF THE SPIDERS ARE STILL THERE, WE MAY BE ABLE TO SAVE YOUR PARENTS!
BUT...WHAT IF THE SPIDERS HAVE ALREADY LEFT?
THEN I SHALL DO EVERYTHING IN MY POWER TO HUNT THEM DOWN...
...EVEN IF I HAVE TO FOLLOW THEM TO THE LORD OF SKULL SPIDERS MYSELF!

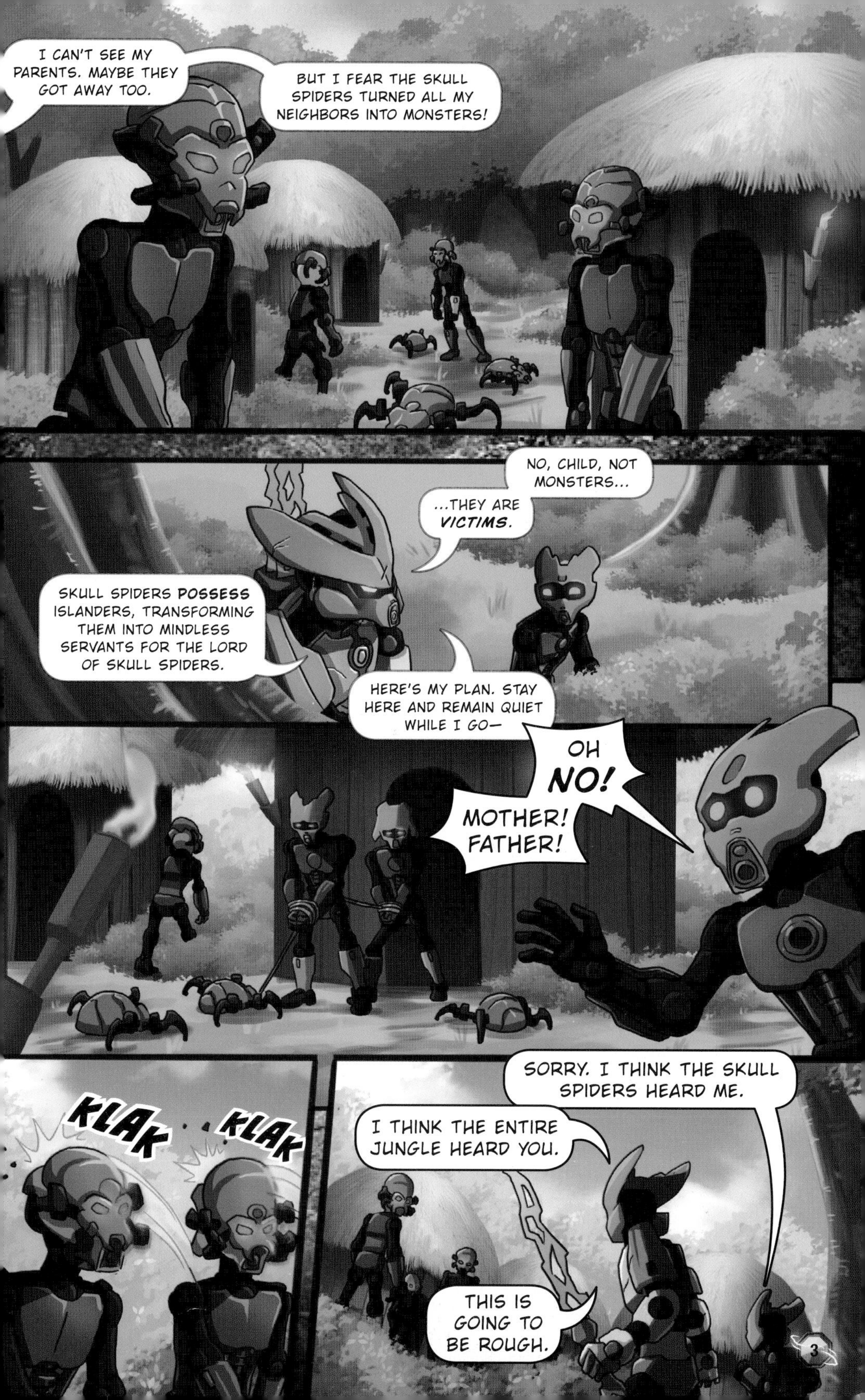
I CAN'T SEE MY PARENTS. MAYBE THEY GOT AWAY TOO.
BUT I FEAR THE SKULL SPIDERS TURNED ALL MY NEIGHBORS INTO MONSTERS!
NO, CHILD, NOT MONSTERS...
...THEY ARE **VICTIMS**.
SKULL SPIDERS **POSSESS** ISLANDERS, TRANSFORMING THEM INTO MINDLESS SERVANTS FOR THE LORD OF SKULL SPIDERS.
HERE'S MY PLAN. STAY HERE AND REMAIN QUIET WHILE I GO—
OH NO!
MOTHER! FATHER!
KLAK
KLAK
SORRY. I THINK THE SKULL SPIDERS HEARD ME.
I THINK THE ENTIRE JUNGLE HEARD YOU.
THIS IS GOING TO BE ROUGH.
3

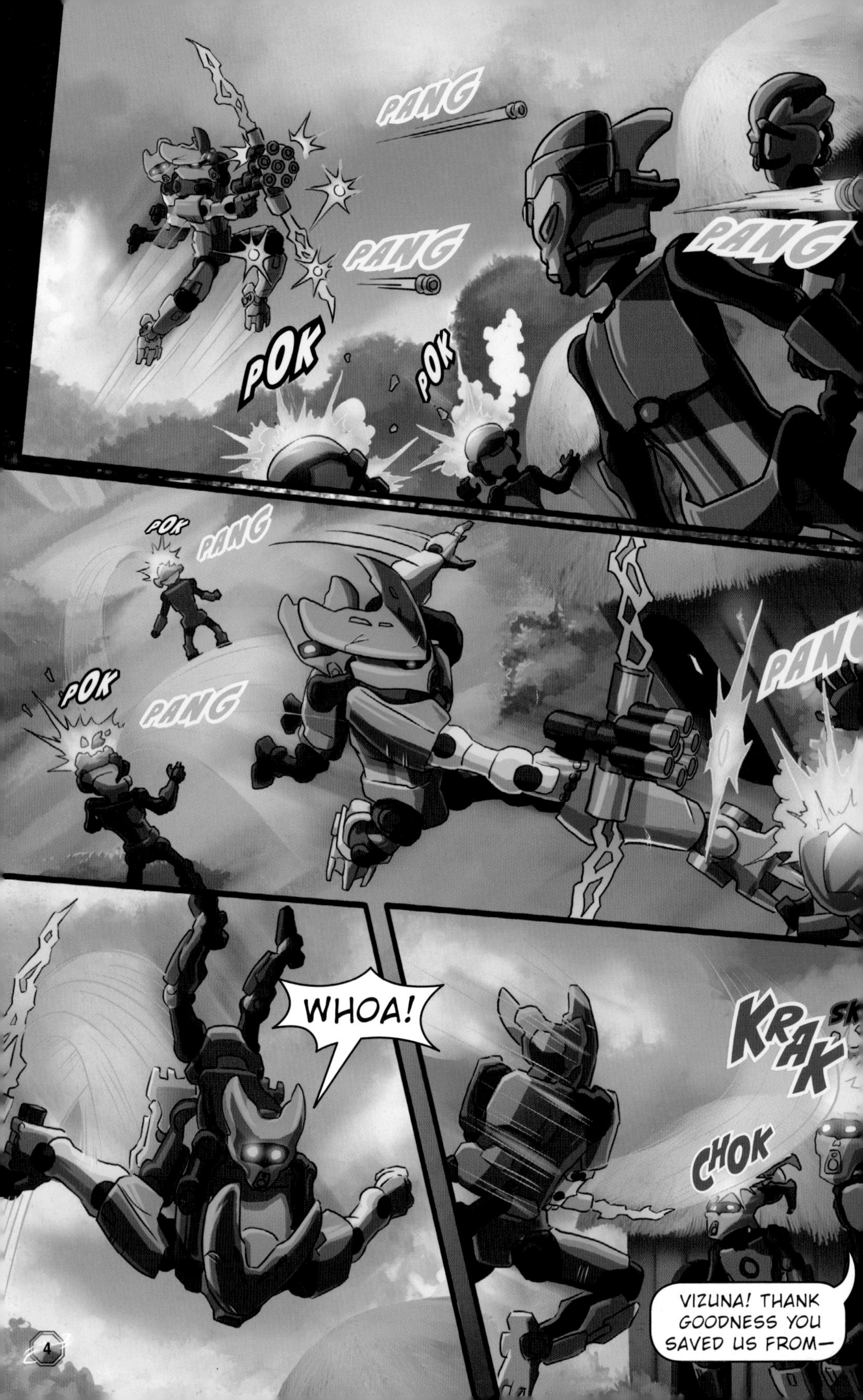
PANG
PANG
PANG
POK
POK
POK
PANG
PANG
POK
PANG
PANG
WHOA!
KRAK
CHOK
VIZUNA! THANK
GOODNESS YOU
SAVED US FROM—

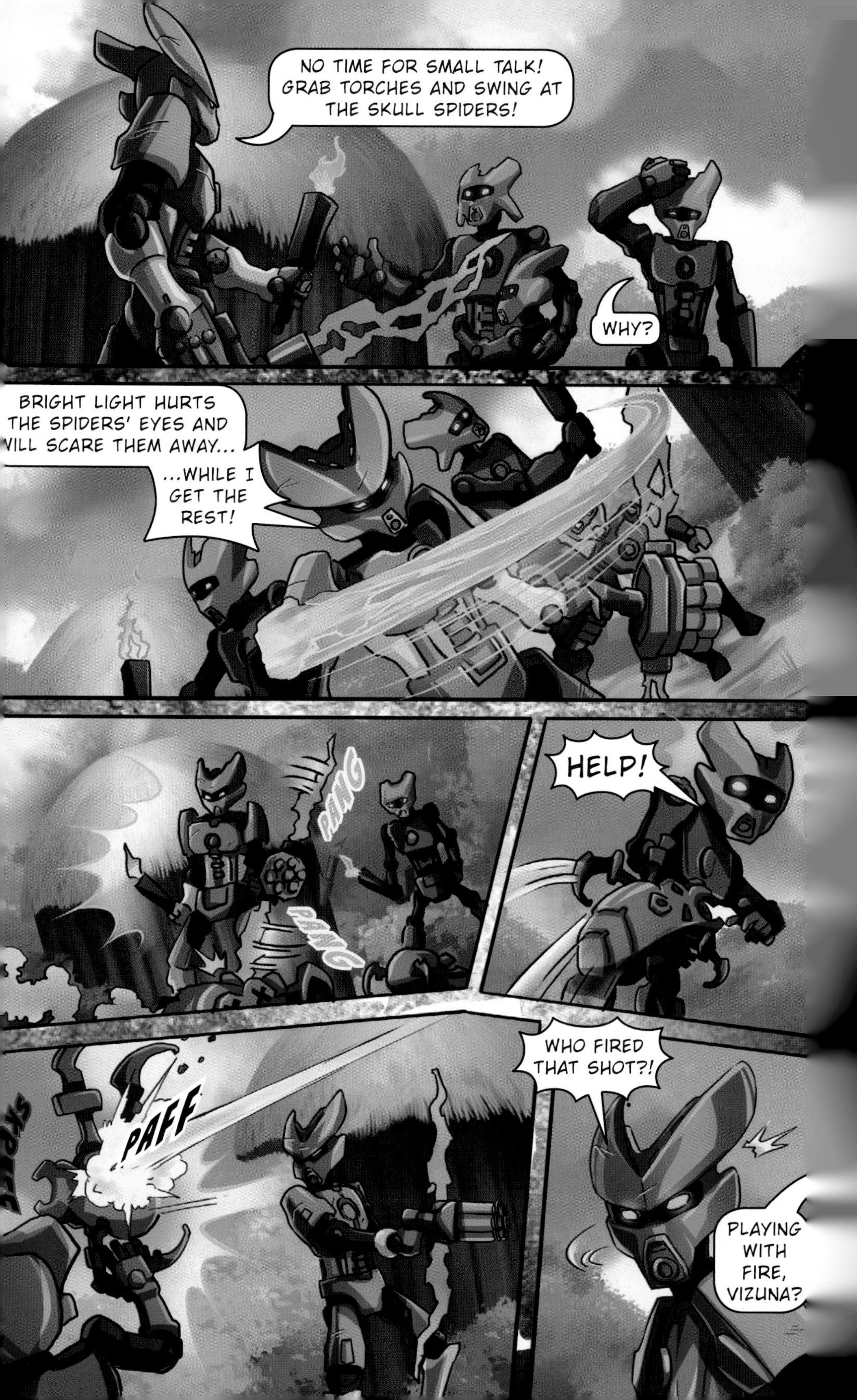
NO TIME FOR SMALL TALK! GRAB TORCHES AND SWING AT THE SKULL SPIDERS!
WHY?
BRIGHT LIGHT HURTS THE SPIDERS' EYES AND WILL SCARE THEM AWAY...
...WHILE I GET THE REST!
PANG
PANG
HELP!
PAFF
WHO FIRED THAT SHOT?!
PLAYING WITH FIRE, VIZUNA?

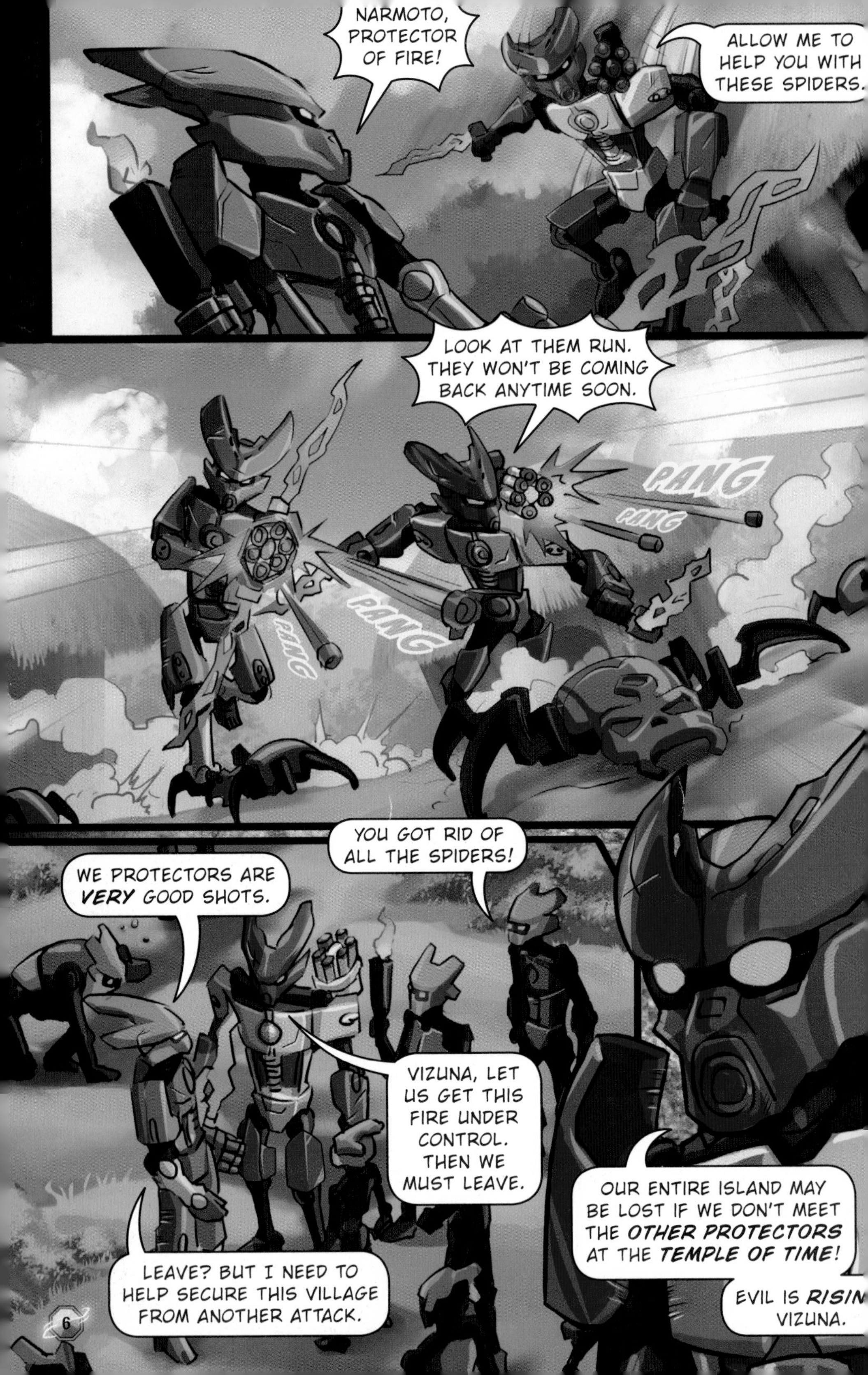
NARMOTO, PROTECTOR OF FIRE!
ALLOW ME TO HELP YOU WITH THESE SPIDERS.
LOOK AT THEM RUN. THEY WON'T BE COMING BACK ANYTIME SOON.
PANG
PANG
PANG
PANG
YOU GOT RID OF ALL THE SPIDERS!
WE PROTECTORS ARE **VERY** GOOD SHOTS.
VIZUNA, LET US GET THIS FIRE UNDER CONTROL. THEN WE MUST LEAVE.
LEAVE? BUT I NEED TO HELP SECURE THIS VILLAGE FROM ANOTHER ATTACK.
OUR ENTIRE ISLAND MAY BE LOST IF WE DON'T MEET THE ***OTHER PROTECTORS*** AT THE ***TEMPLE OF TIME***!
EVIL IS ***RISIN***
VIZUNA.

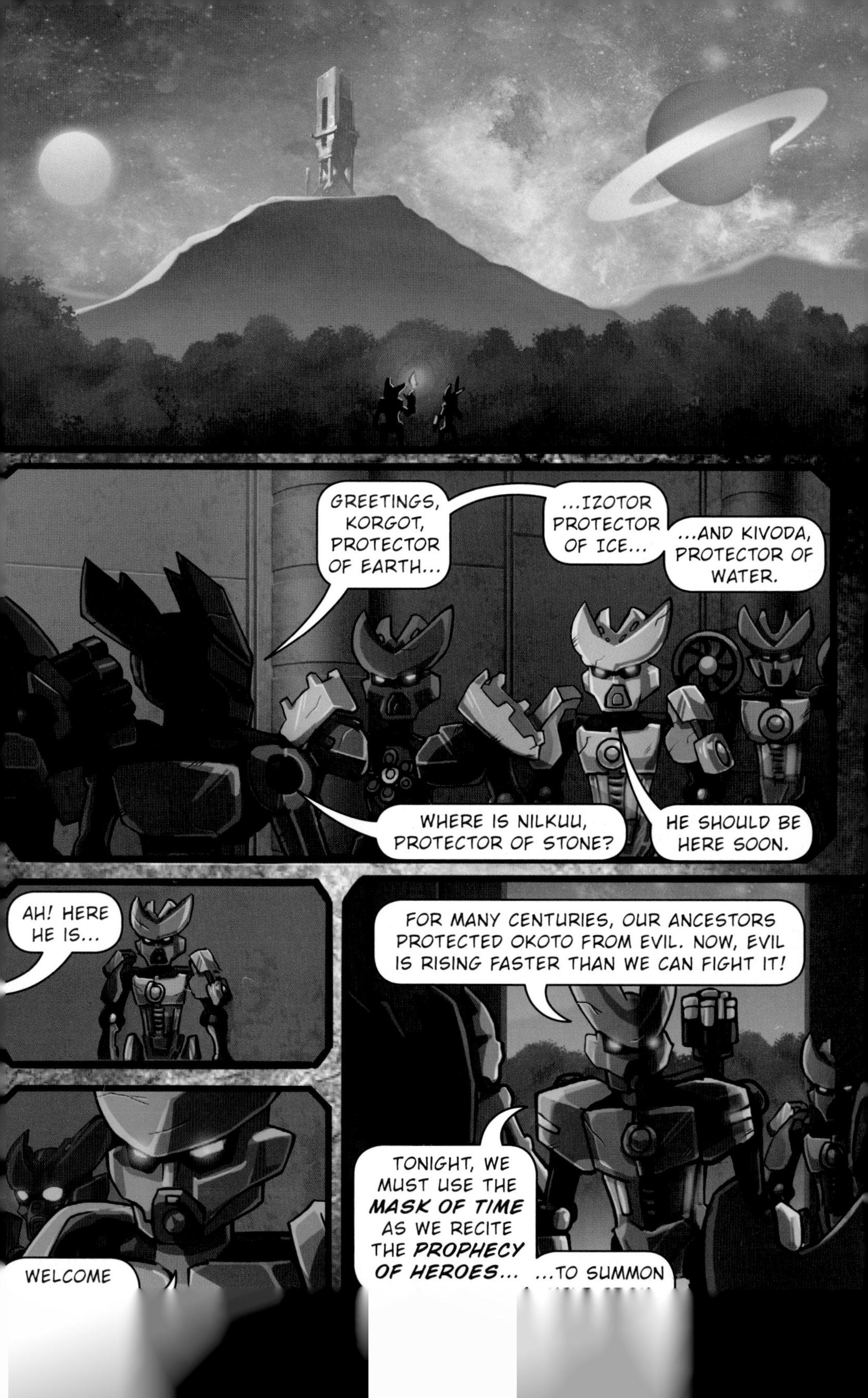
GREETINGS, KORGOT, PROTECTOR OF EARTH...
...IZOTOR PROTECTOR OF ICE...
...AND KIVODA, PROTECTOR OF WATER.
WHERE IS NILKUU, PROTECTOR OF STONE?
HE SHOULD BE HERE SOON.
AH! HERE HE IS...
FOR MANY CENTURIES, OUR ANCESTORS PROTECTED OKOTO FROM EVIL. NOW, EVIL IS RISING FASTER THAN WE CAN FIGHT IT!
WELCOME
TONIGHT, WE MUST USE THE MASK OF TIME AS WE RECITE THE PROPHECY OF HEROES...
...TO SUMMON

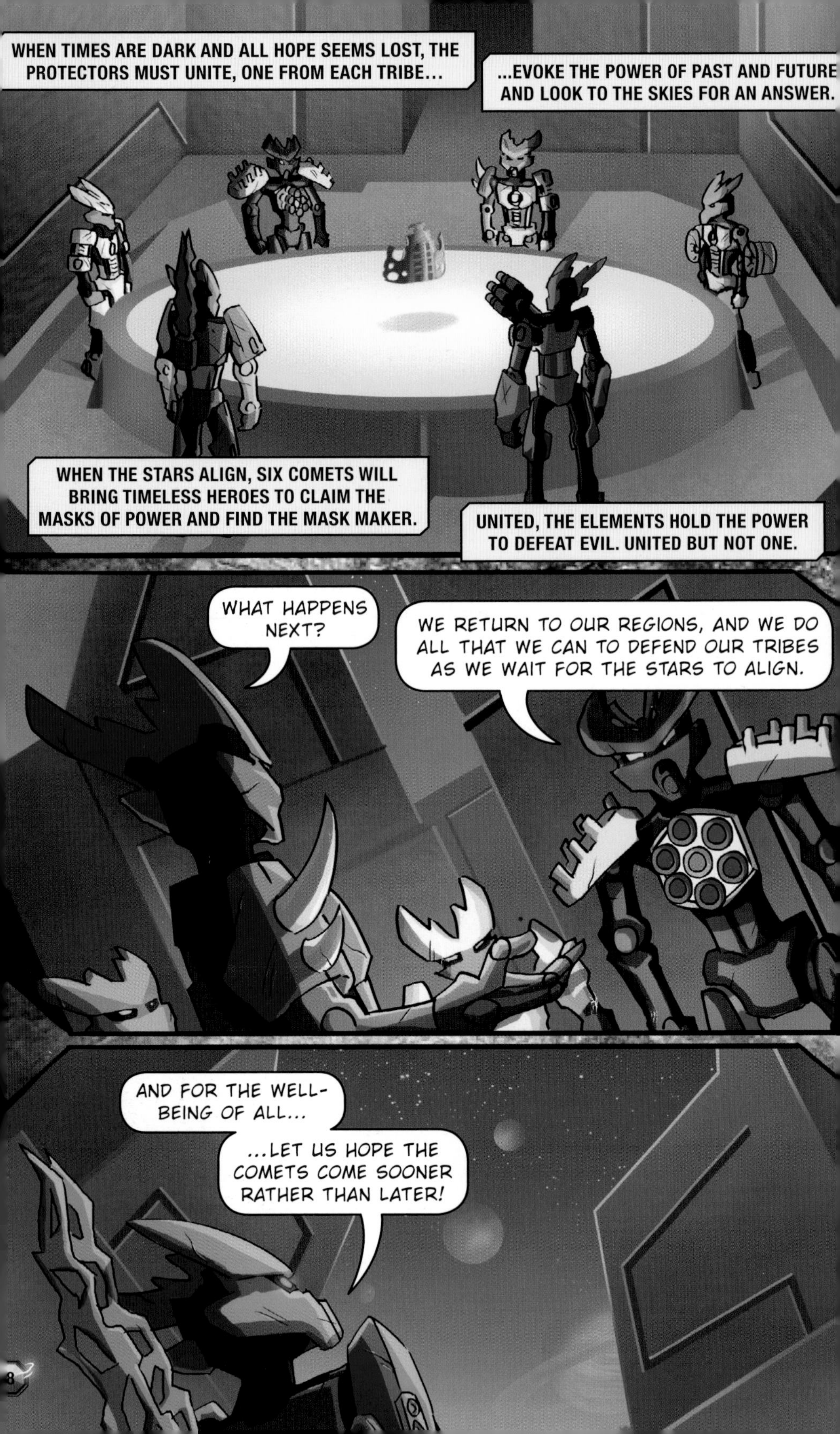
WHEN TIMES ARE DARK AND ALL HOPE SEEMS LOST, THE PROTECTORS MUST UNITE, ONE FROM EACH TRIBE…
...EVOKE THE POWER OF PAST AND FUTURE AND LOOK TO THE SKIES FOR AN ANSWER.
WHEN THE STARS ALIGN, SIX COMETS WILL BRING TIMELESS HEROES TO CLAIM THE MASKS OF POWER AND FIND THE MASK MAKER.
UNITED, THE ELEMENTS HOLD THE POWER TO DEFEAT EVIL. UNITED BUT NOT ONE.
WHAT HAPPENS NEXT?
WE RETURN TO OUR REGIONS, AND WE DO ALL THAT WE CAN TO DEFEND OUR TRIBES AS WE WAIT FOR THE STARS TO ALIGN.
AND FOR THE WELL-BEING OF ALL...
...LET US HOPE THE COMETS COME SOONER RATHER THAN LATER!

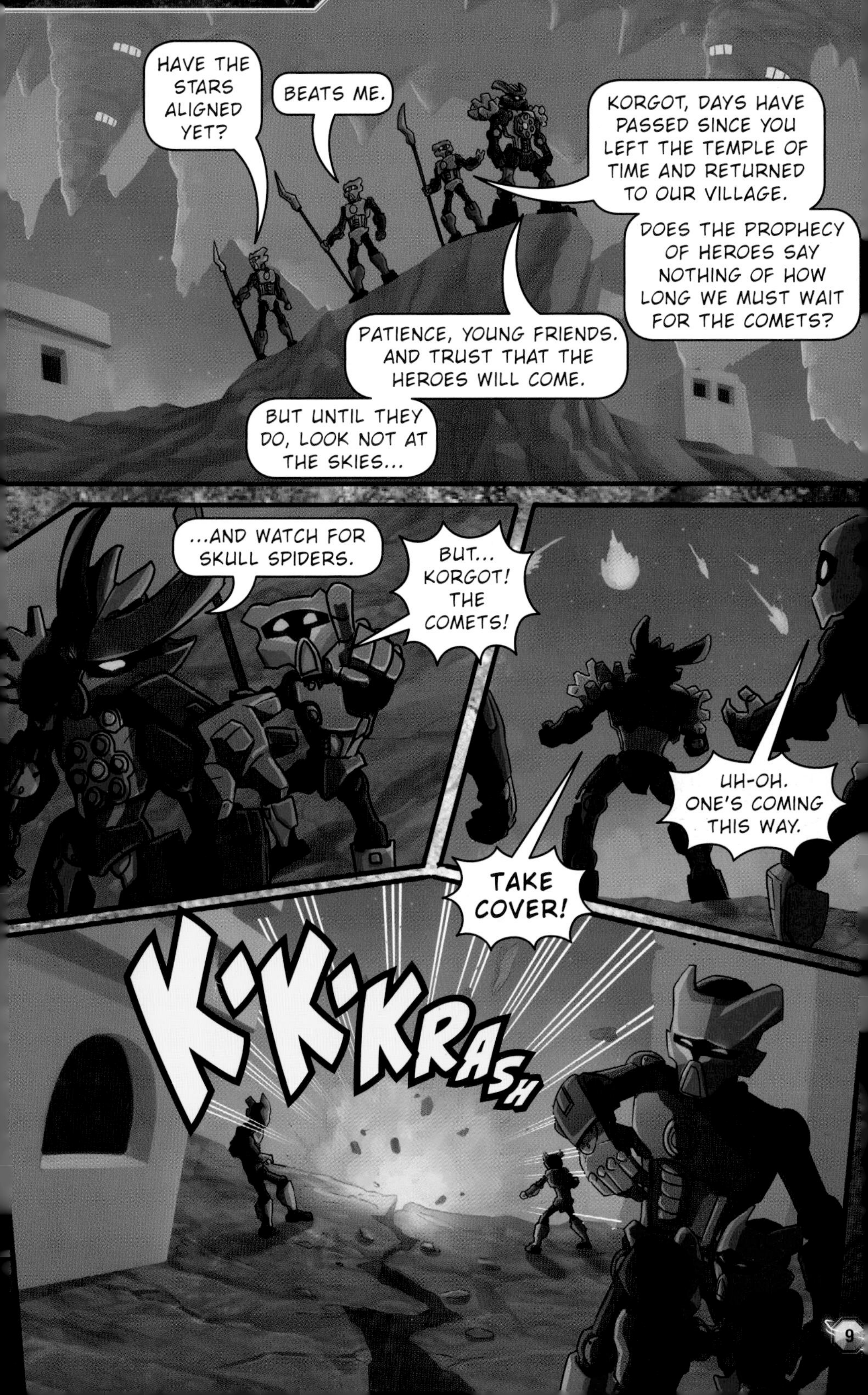
HAVE THE STARS ALIGNED YET?
BEATS ME.
KORGOT, DAYS HAVE PASSED SINCE YOU LEFT THE TEMPLE OF TIME AND RETURNED TO OUR VILLAGE.
DOES THE PROPHECY OF HEROES SAY NOTHING OF HOW LONG WE MUST WAIT FOR THE COMETS?
PATIENCE, YOUNG FRIENDS. AND TRUST THAT THE HEROES WILL COME.
BUT UNTIL THEY DO, LOOK NOT AT THE SKIES...
...AND WATCH FOR SKULL SPIDERS.
BUT... KORGOT! THE COMETS!
UH-OH. ONE'S COMING THIS WAY.
TAKE COVER!
K-K-KRASH

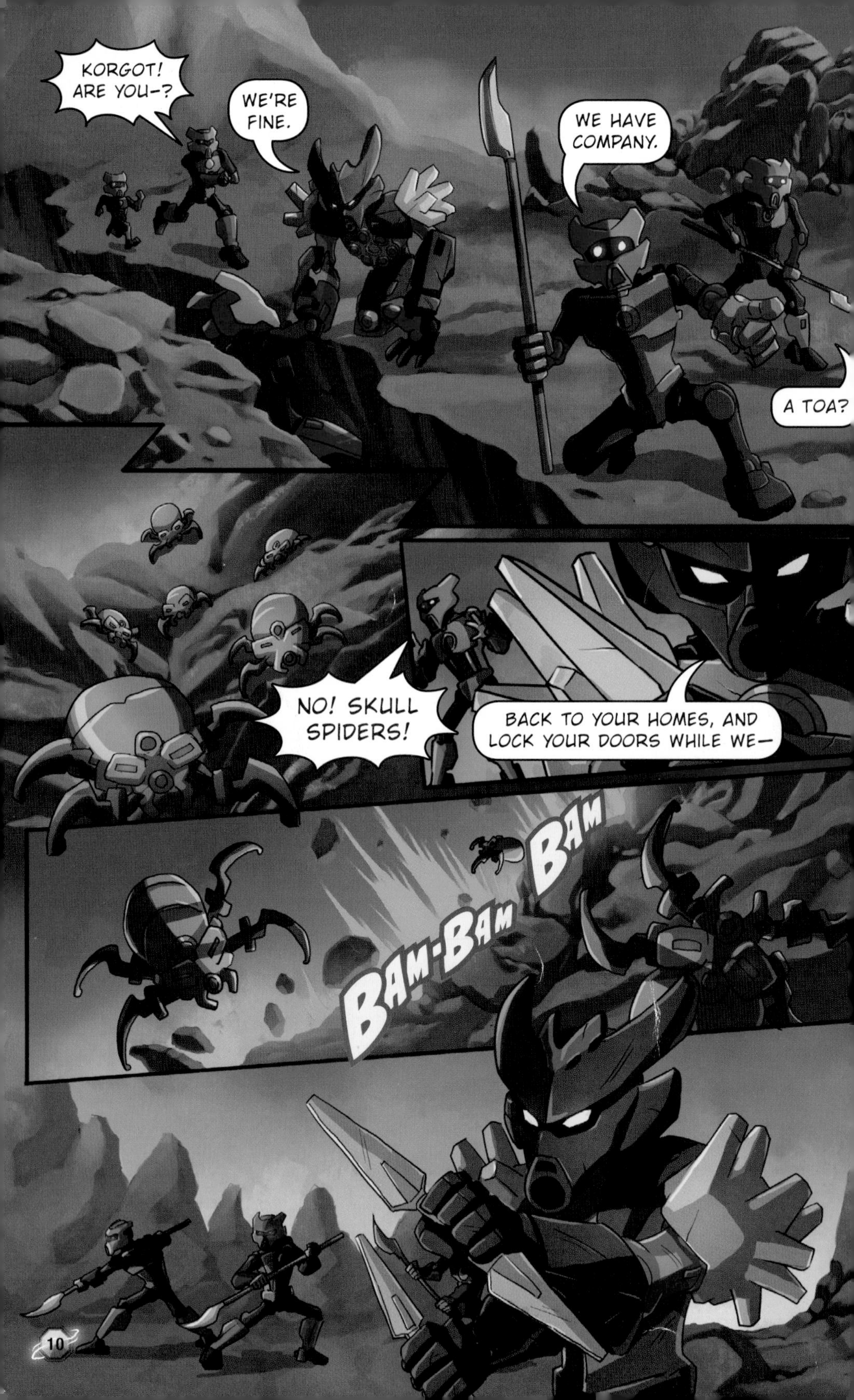
KORGOT! ARE YOU-?
WE'RE FINE.
WE HAVE COMPANY.
A TOA?
NO! SKULL SPIDERS!
BACK TO YOUR HOMES, AND LOCK YOUR DOORS WHILE WE—
BAM-BAM BAM

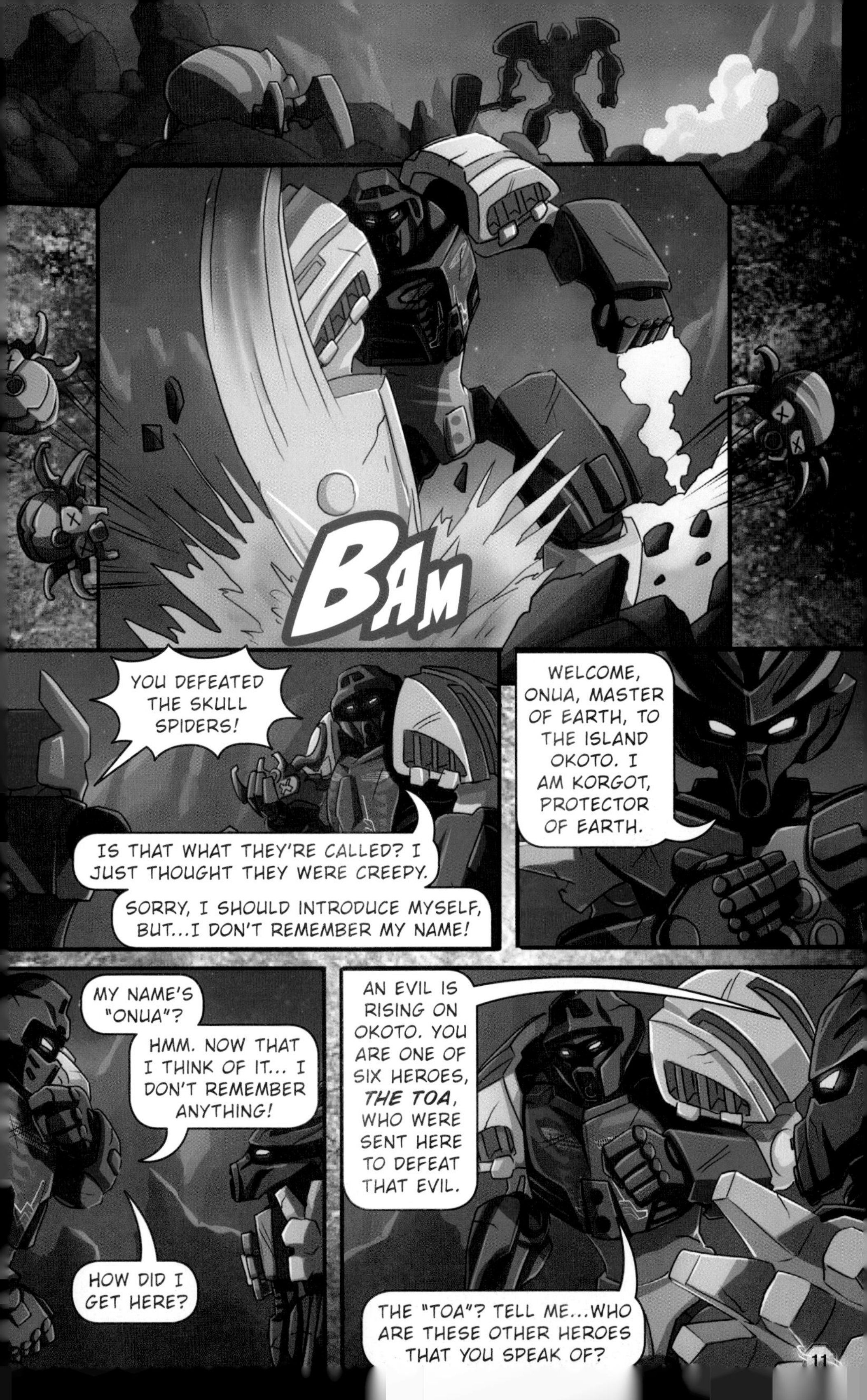
BAM
YOU DEFEATED THE SKULL SPIDERS!
IS THAT WHAT THEY'RE CALLED? I JUST THOUGHT THEY WERE CREEPY.
SORRY, I SHOULD INTRODUCE MYSELF, BUT...I DON'T REMEMBER MY NAME!
WELCOME, ONUA, MASTER OF EARTH, TO THE ISLAND OKOTO. I AM KORGOT, PROTECTOR OF EARTH.
MY NAME'S "ONUA"?
HMM. NOW THAT I THINK OF IT... I DON'T REMEMBER ANYTHING!
HOW DID I GET HERE?
AN EVIL IS RISING ON OKOTO. YOU ARE ONE OF SIX HEROES, THE TOA, WHO WERE SENT HERE TO DEFEAT THAT EVIL.
THE "TOA"? TELL ME...WHO ARE THESE OTHER HEROES THAT YOU SPEAK OF?

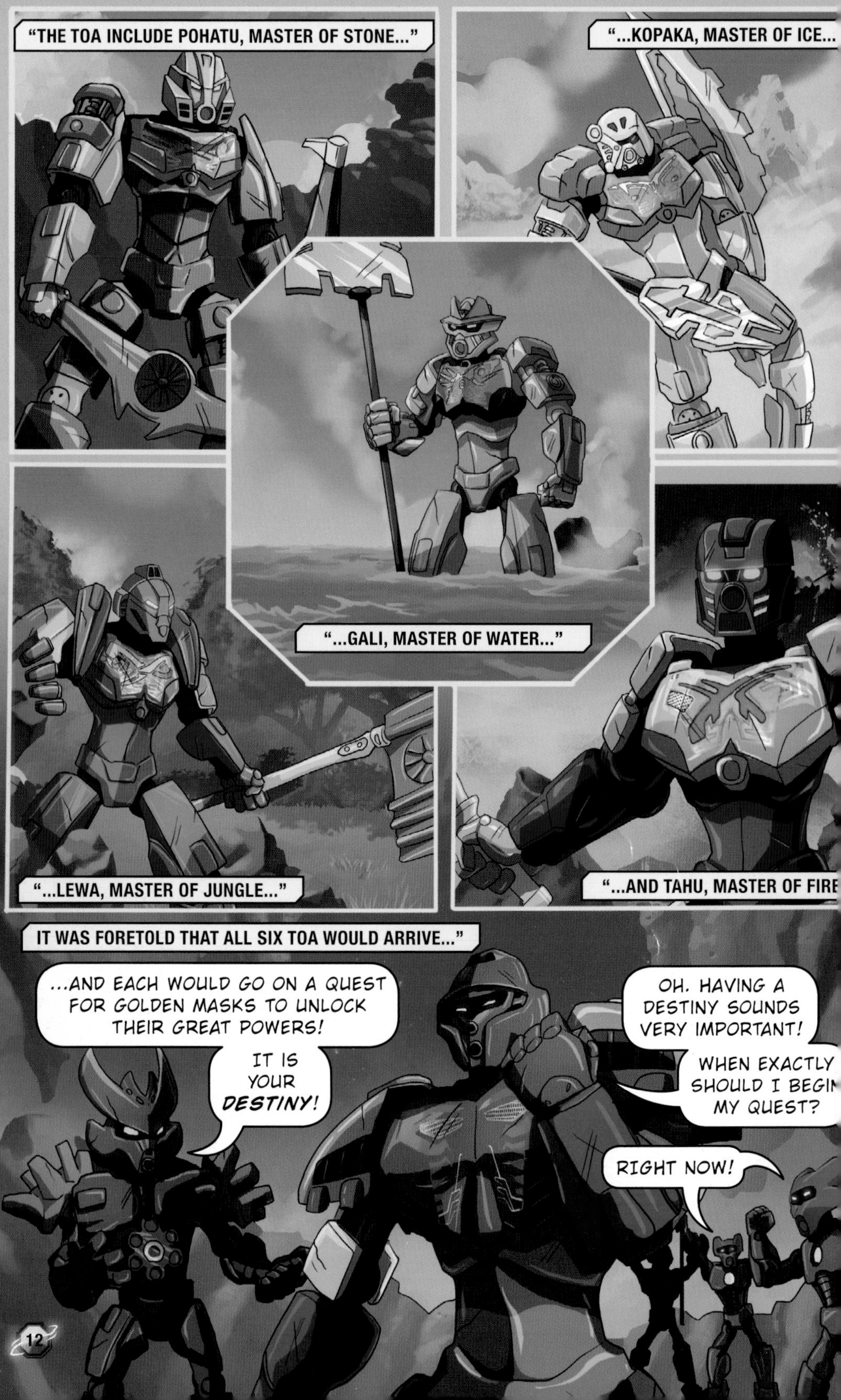
"THE TOA INCLUDE POHATU, MASTER OF STONE..."
"...KOPAKA, MASTER OF ICE...
"...GALI, MASTER OF WATER..."
"...LEWA, MASTER OF JUNGLE..."
"...AND TAHU, MASTER OF FIRE
IT WAS FORETOLD THAT ALL SIX TOA WOULD ARRIVE..."
...AND EACH WOULD GO ON A QUEST FOR GOLDEN MASKS TO UNLOCK THEIR GREAT POWERS!
IT IS YOUR DESTINY!
OH. HAVING A DESTINY SOUNDS VERY IMPORTANT!
WHEN EXACTLY SHOULD I BEGIN MY QUEST?
RIGHT NOW!

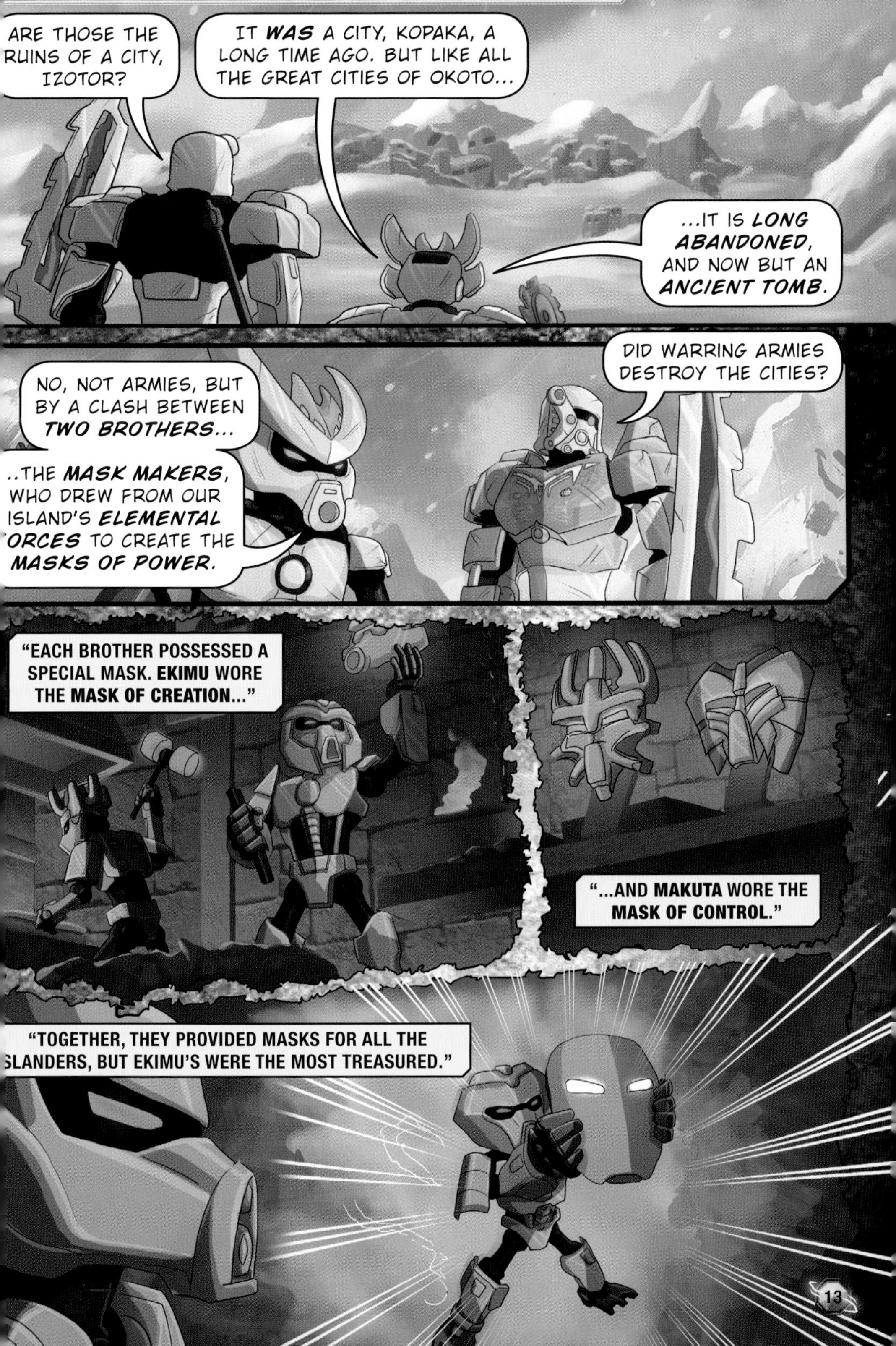
ARE THOSE THE RUINS OF A CITY, IZOTOR?
IT WAS A CITY, KOPAKA, A LONG TIME AGO. BUT LIKE ALL THE GREAT CITIES OF OKOTO...
...IT IS LONG ABANDONED, AND NOW BUT AN ANCIENT TOMB.
DID WARRING ARMIES DESTROY THE CITIES?
NO, NOT ARMIES, BUT BY A CLASH BETWEEN TWO BROTHERS...
..THE MASK MAKERS, WHO DREW FROM OUR ISLAND'S ELEMENTAL ORCES TO CREATE THE MASKS OF POWER.
"EACH BROTHER POSSESSED A SPECIAL MASK. EKIMU WORE THE MASK OF CREATION..."
"...AND MAKUTA WORE THE MASK OF CONTROL."
"TOGETHER, THEY PROVIDED MASKS FOR ALL THE SLANDERS, BUT EKIMU'S WERE THE MOST TREASURED."

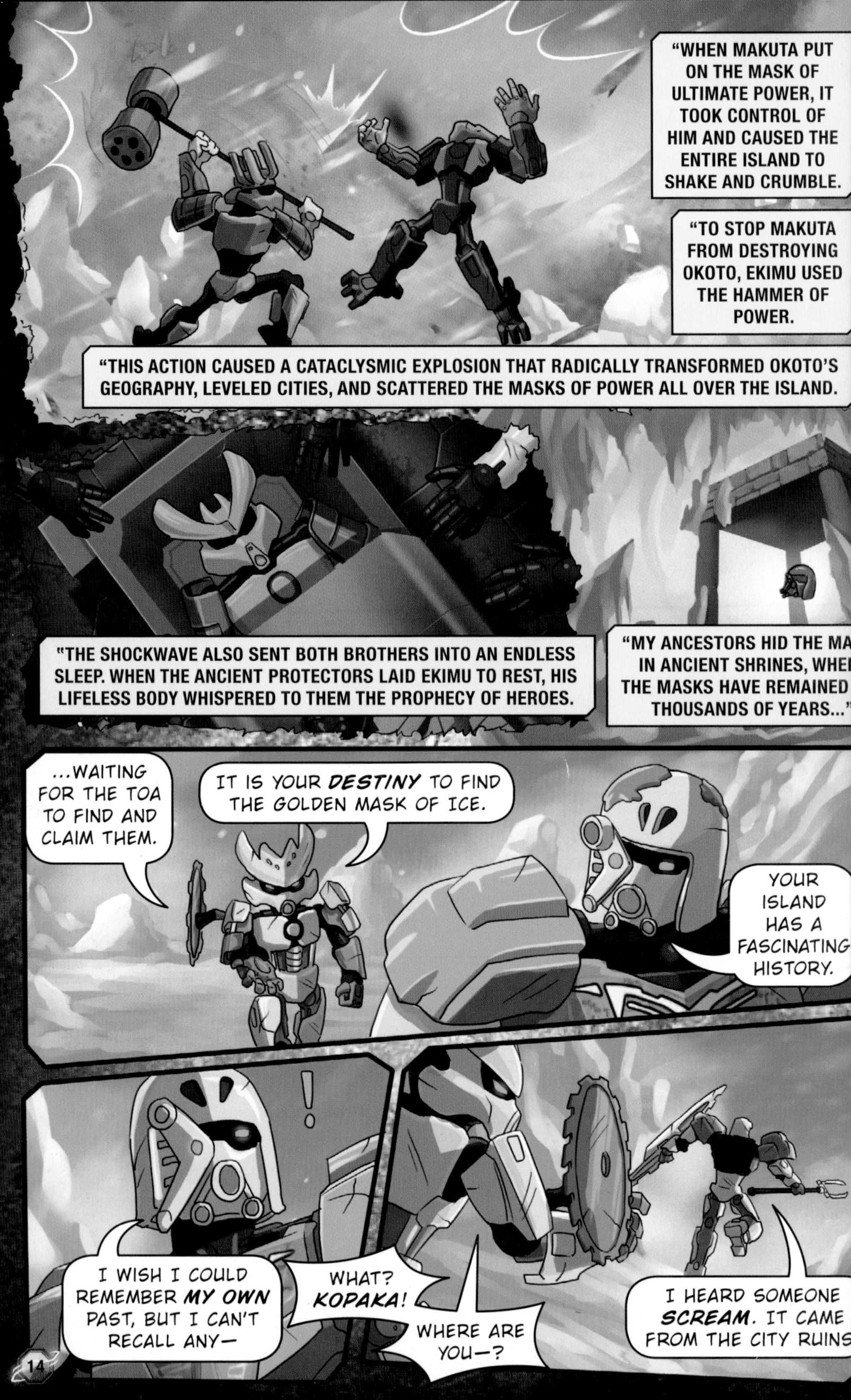
"WHEN MAKUTA PUT ON THE MASK OF ULTIMATE POWER, IT TOOK CONTROL OF HIM AND CAUSED THE ENTIRE ISLAND TO SHAKE AND CRUMBLE.
"TO STOP MAKUTA FROM DESTROYING OKOTO, EKIMU USED THE HAMMER OF POWER.
"THIS ACTION CAUSED A CATACLYSMIC EXPLOSION THAT RADICALLY TRANSFORMED OKOTO'S GEOGRAPHY, LEVELED CITIES, AND SCATTERED THE MASKS OF POWER ALL OVER THE ISLAND.
"THE SHOCKWAVE ALSO SENT BOTH BROTHERS INTO AN ENDLESS SLEEP. WHEN THE ANCIENT PROTECTORS LAID EKIMU TO REST, HIS LIFELESS BODY WHISPERED TO THEM THE PROPHECY OF HEROES.
"MY ANCESTORS HID THE MA IN ANCIENT SHRINES, WHE THE MASKS HAVE REMAINED THOUSANDS OF YEARS..."
...WAITING FOR THE TOA TO FIND AND CLAIM THEM.
IT IS YOUR *DESTINY* TO FIND THE GOLDEN MASK OF ICE.
YOUR ISLAND HAS A FASCINATING HISTORY.
!
I WISH I COULD REMEMBER **MY OWN** PAST, BUT I CAN'T RECALL ANY—
WHAT? ***KOPAKA!***
WHERE ARE YOU—?
I HEARD SOMEONE ***SCREAM***. IT CAME FROM THE CITY RUINS

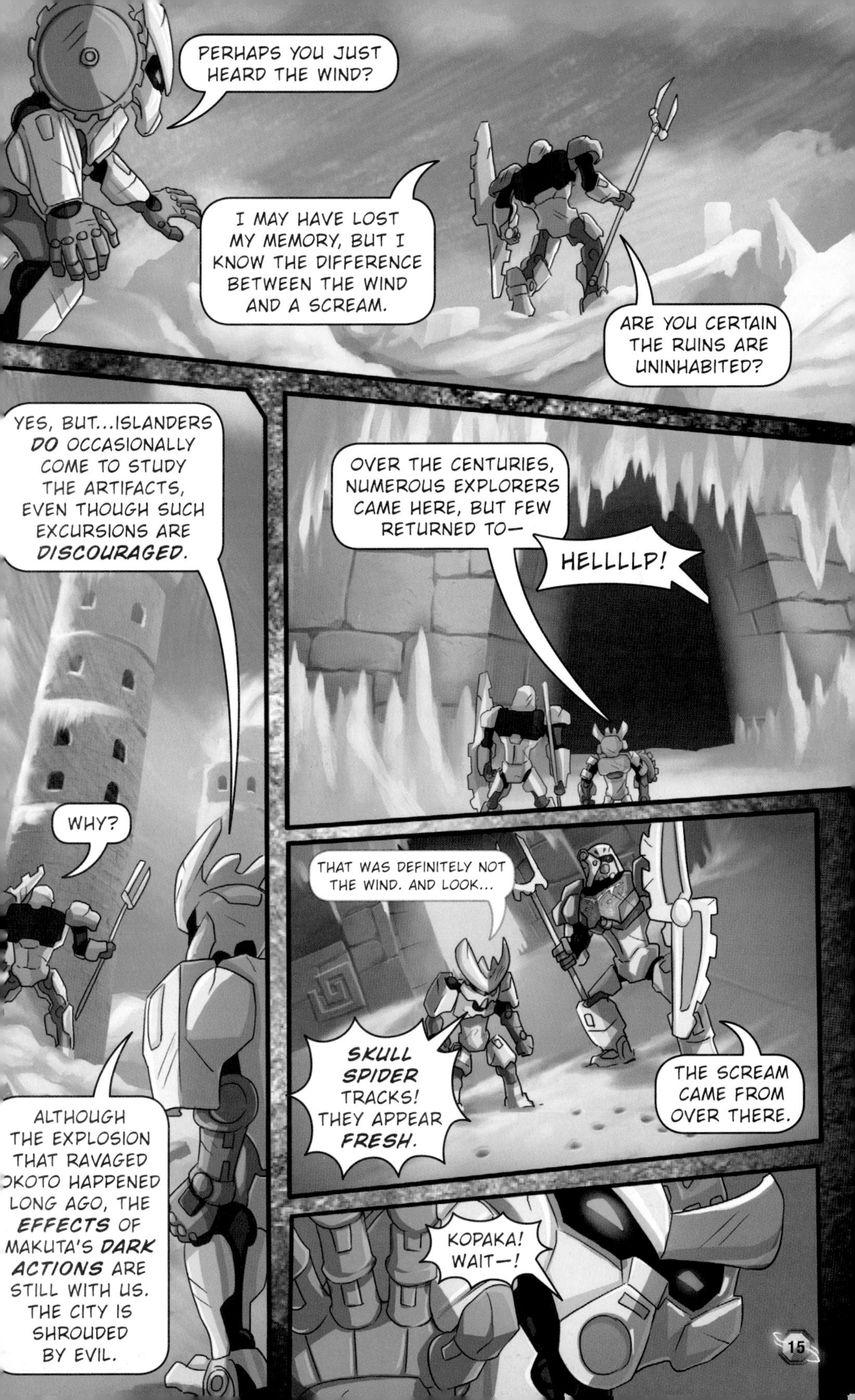
PERHAPS YOU JUST HEARD THE WIND?
I MAY HAVE LOST MY MEMORY, BUT I KNOW THE DIFFERENCE BETWEEN THE WIND AND A SCREAM.
ARE YOU CERTAIN THE RUINS ARE UNINHABITED?
YES, BUT...ISLANDERS DO OCCASIONALLY COME TO STUDY THE ARTIFACTS, EVEN THOUGH SUCH EXCURSIONS ARE DISCOURAGED.
WHY?
ALTHOUGH THE EXPLOSION THAT RAVAGED OKOTO HAPPENED LONG AGO, THE EFFECTS OF MAKUTA'S DARK ACTIONS ARE STILL WITH US. THE CITY IS SHROUDED BY EVIL.
OVER THE CENTURIES, NUMEROUS EXPLORERS CAME HERE, BUT FEW RETURNED TO—
HELLLLP!
THAT WAS DEFINITELY NOT THE WIND. AND LOOK...
SKULL SPIDER TRACKS! THEY APPEAR FRESH.
THE SCREAM CAME FROM OVER THERE.
KOPAKA! WAIT—!

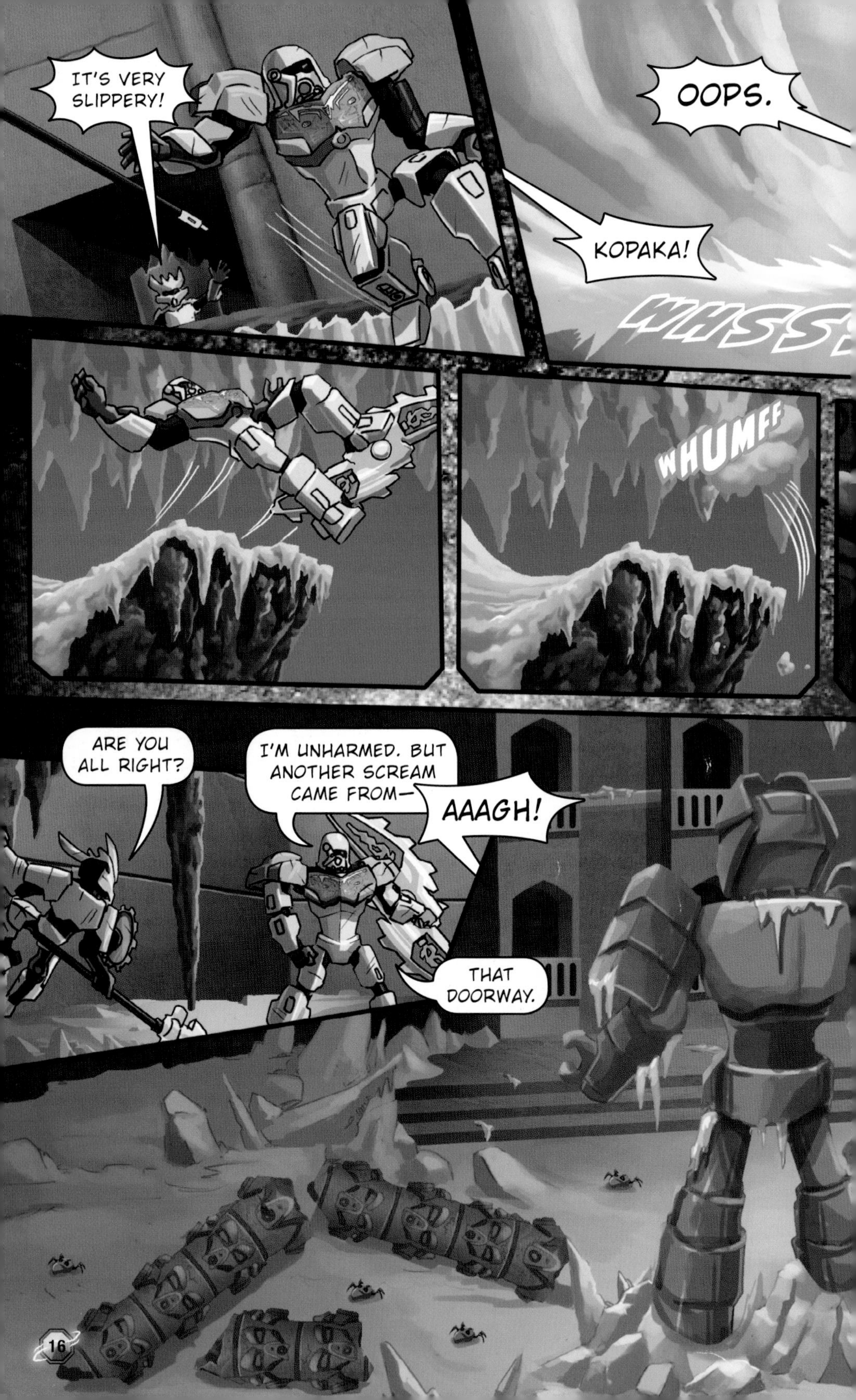
IT'S VERY SLIPPERY!
OOPS.
KOPAKA!
WHSS
WHUMFF
ARE YOU ALL RIGHT?
I'M UNHARMED. BUT ANOTHER SCREAM CAME FROM—
AAAGH!
THAT DOORWAY.

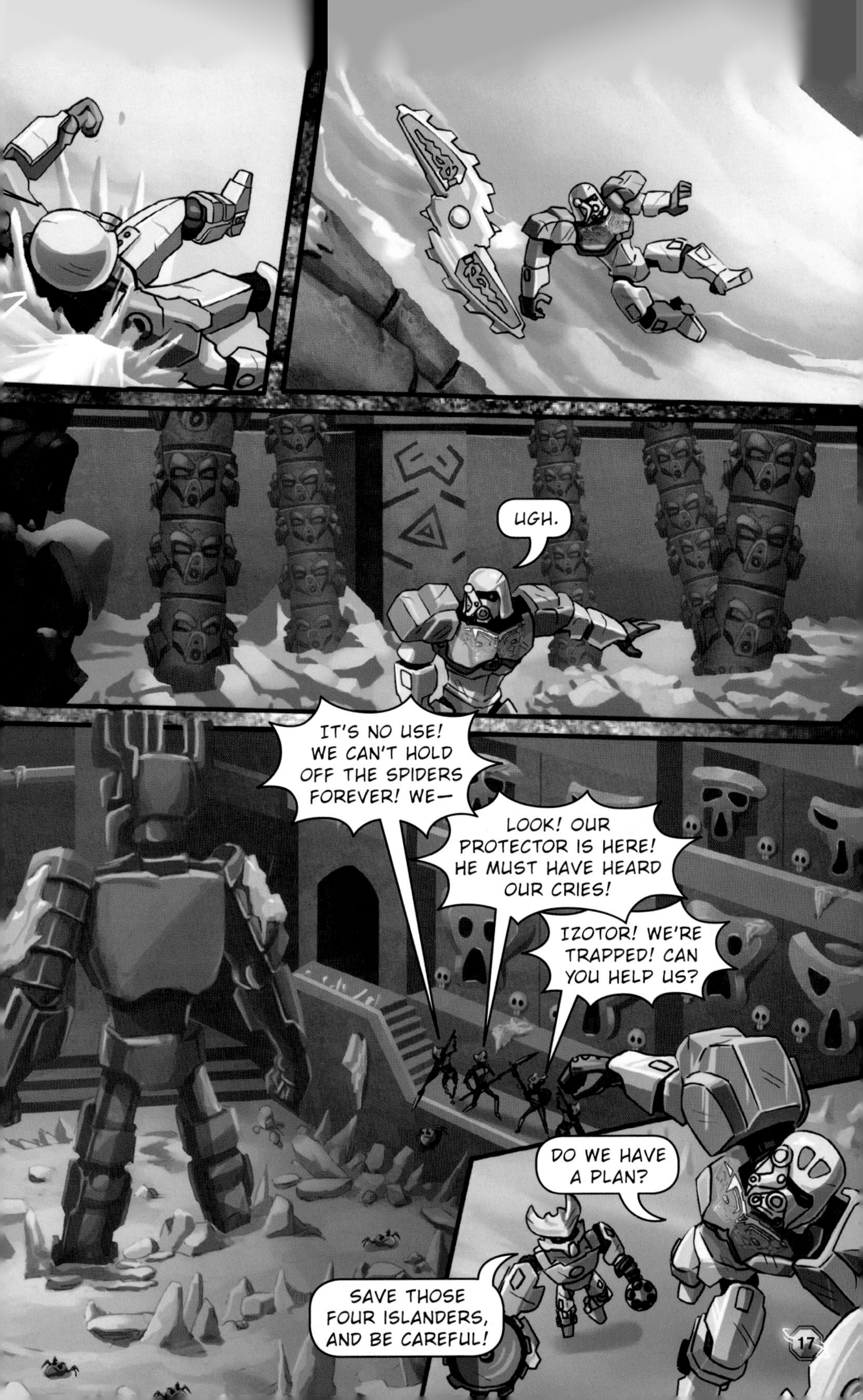
UGH.
IT'S NO USE! WE CAN'T HOLD OFF THE SPIDERS FOREVER! WE—
LOOK! OUR PROTECTOR IS HERE! HE MUST HAVE HEARD OUR CRIES!
IZOTOR! WE'RE TRAPPED! CAN YOU HELP US?
DO WE HAVE A PLAN?
SAVE THOSE FOUR ISLANDERS, AND BE CAREFUL!

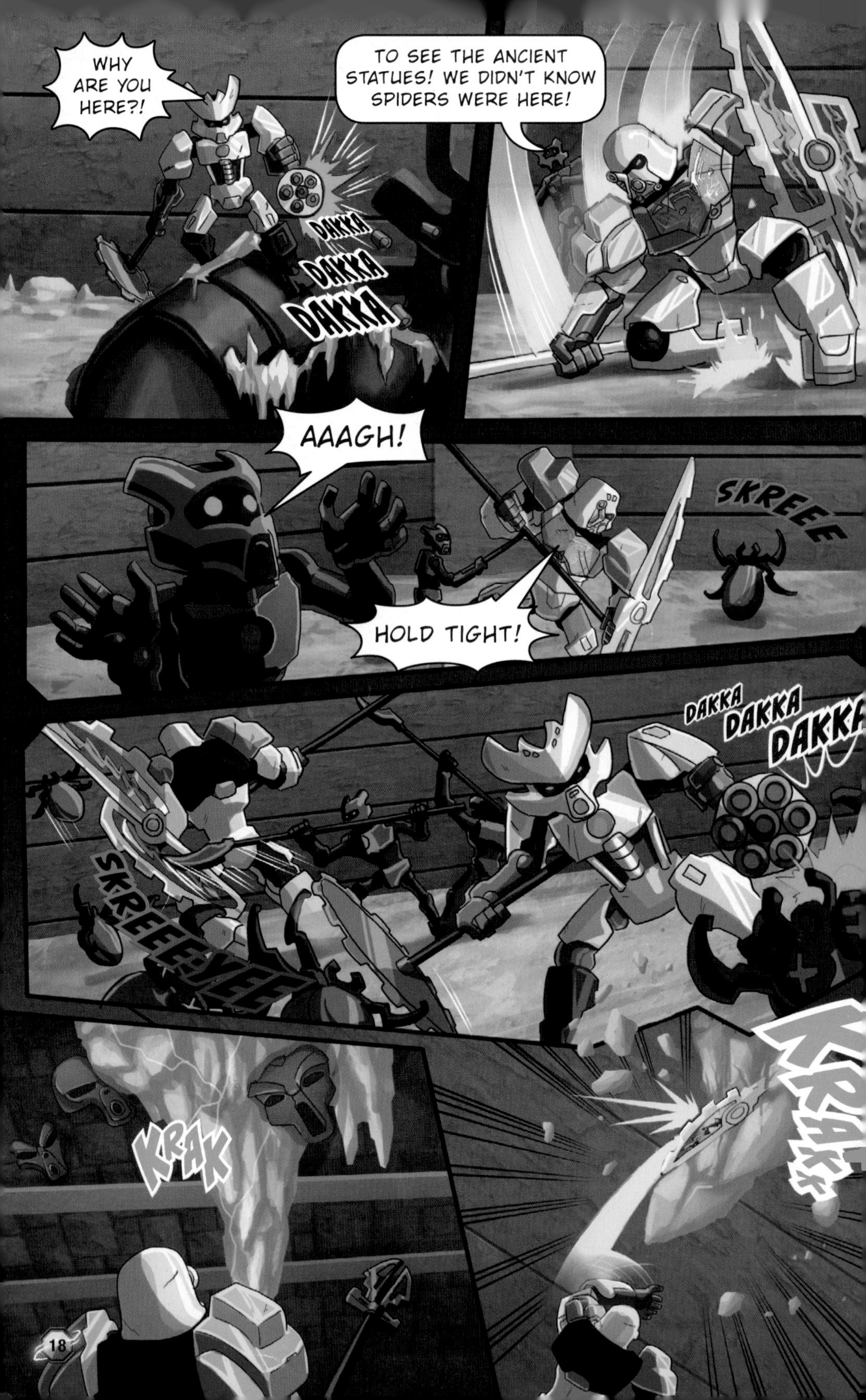
WHY ARE YOU HERE?!
TO SEE THE ANCIENT STATUES! WE DIDN'T KNOW SPIDERS WERE HERE!
DAKKA
DAKKA
DAKKA
AAAGH!
SKREEE
HOLD TIGHT!
DAKKA
DAKKA
DAKKA
SKREEEEEE
KRAK
KRAK

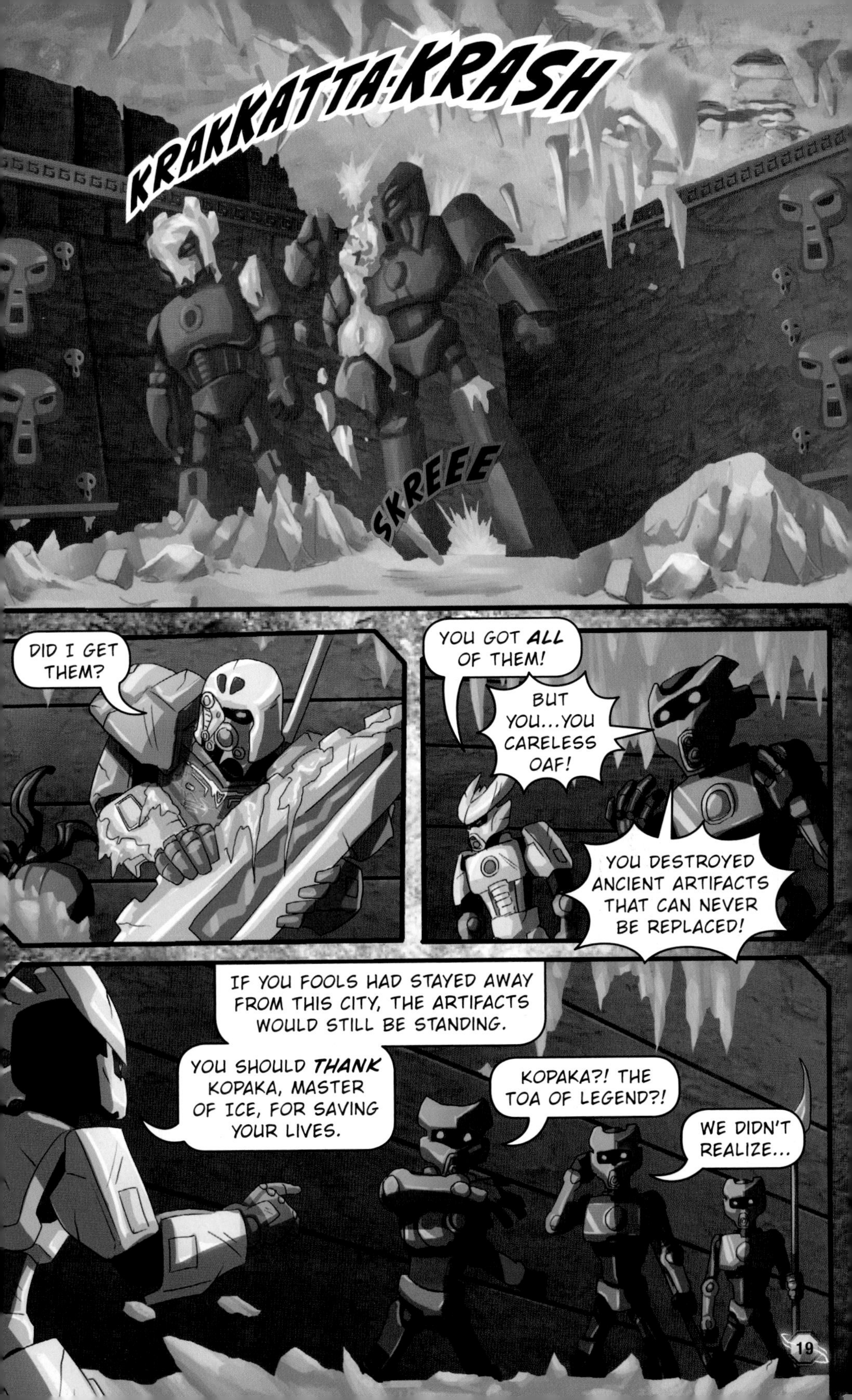
KRAKKATTA-KRASH
SKREEE
DID I GET THEM?
YOU GOT ALL OF THEM!
BUT YOU...YOU CARELESS OAF!
YOU DESTROYED ANCIENT ARTIFACTS THAT CAN NEVER BE REPLACED!
IF YOU FOOLS HAD STAYED AWAY FROM THIS CITY, THE ARTIFACTS WOULD STILL BE STANDING.
YOU SHOULD THANK KOPAKA, MASTER OF ICE, FOR SAVING YOUR LIVES.
KOPAKA?! THE TOA OF LEGEND?!
WE DIDN'T REALIZE...

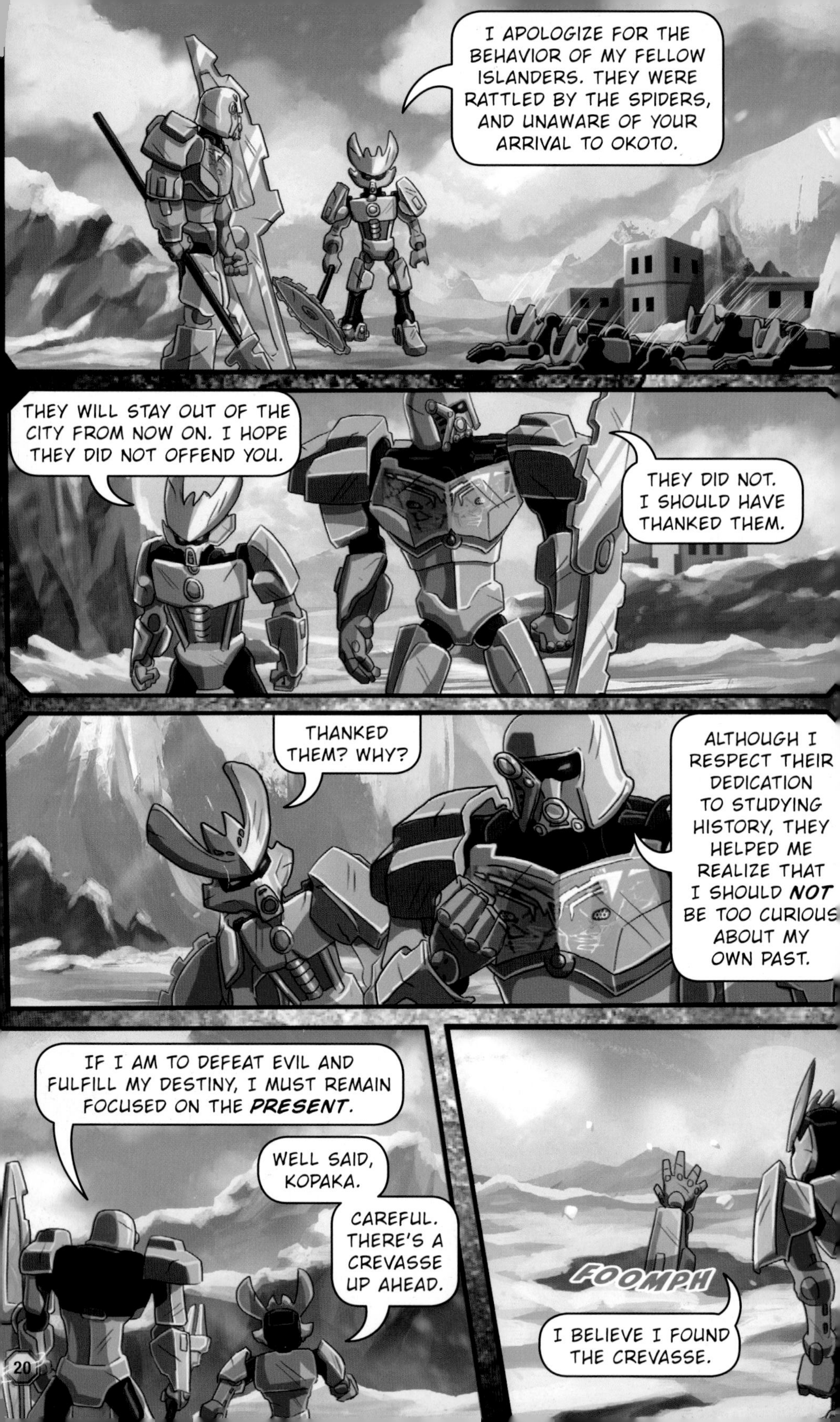
I APOLOGIZE FOR THE BEHAVIOR OF MY FELLOW ISLANDERS. THEY WERE RATTLED BY THE SPIDERS, AND UNAWARE OF YOUR ARRIVAL TO OKOTO.
THEY WILL STAY OUT OF THE CITY FROM NOW ON. I HOPE THEY DID NOT OFFEND YOU.
THEY DID NOT. I SHOULD HAVE THANKED THEM.
THANKED THEM? WHY?
ALTHOUGH I RESPECT THEIR DEDICATION TO STUDYING HISTORY, THEY HELPED ME REALIZE THAT I SHOULD NOT BE TOO CURIOUS ABOUT MY OWN PAST.
IF I AM TO DEFEAT EVIL AND FULFILL MY DESTINY, I MUST REMAIN FOCUSED ON THE PRESENT.
WELL SAID, KOPAKA.
CAREFUL. THERE'S A CREVASSE UP AHEAD.
FOOMPH
I BELIEVE I FOUND THE CREVASSE.

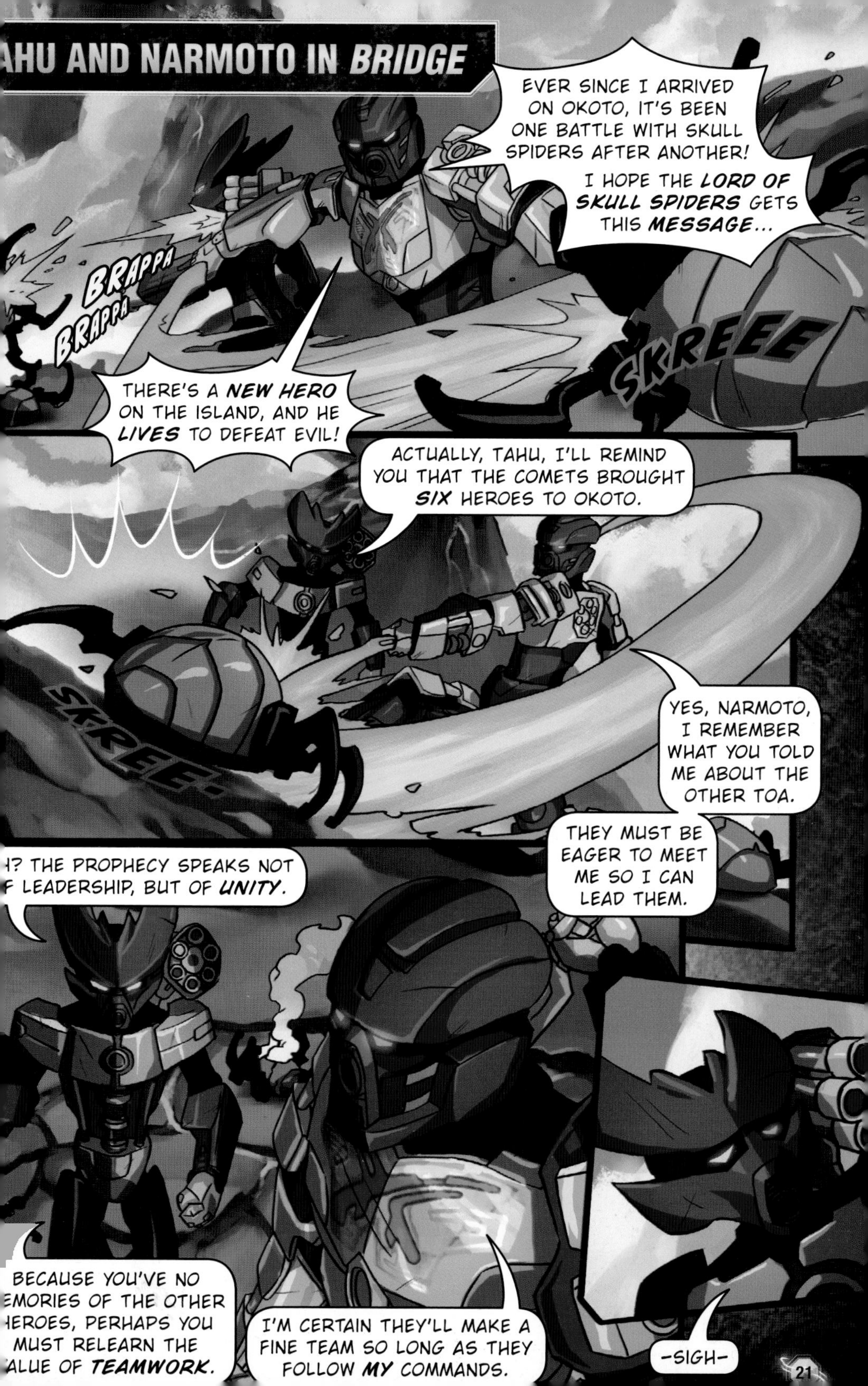

AHU AND NARMOTO IN BRIDGE
EVER SINCE I ARRIVED ON OKOTO, IT'S BEEN ONE BATTLE WITH SKULL SPIDERS AFTER ANOTHER!
I HOPE THE LORD OF SKULL SPIDERS GETS THIS MESSAGE...
BRAPPA BRAPPA
THERE'S A NEW HERO ON THE ISLAND, AND HE LIVES TO DEFEAT EVIL!
SKREEE
ACTUALLY, TAHU, I'LL REMIND YOU THAT THE COMETS BROUGHT SIX HEROES TO OKOTO.
SKREEE
YES, NARMOTO, I REMEMBER WHAT YOU TOLD ME ABOUT THE OTHER TOA.
THEY MUST BE EAGER TO MEET ME SO I CAN LEAD THEM.
? THE PROPHECY SPEAKS NOT LEADERSHIP, BUT OF UNITY.
BECAUSE YOU'VE NO EMORIES OF THE OTHER HEROES, PERHAPS YOU MUST RELEARN THE ALUE OF TEAMWORK.
I'M CERTAIN THEY'LL MAKE A FINE TEAM SO LONG AS THEY FOLLOW MY COMMANDS.
-SIGH-

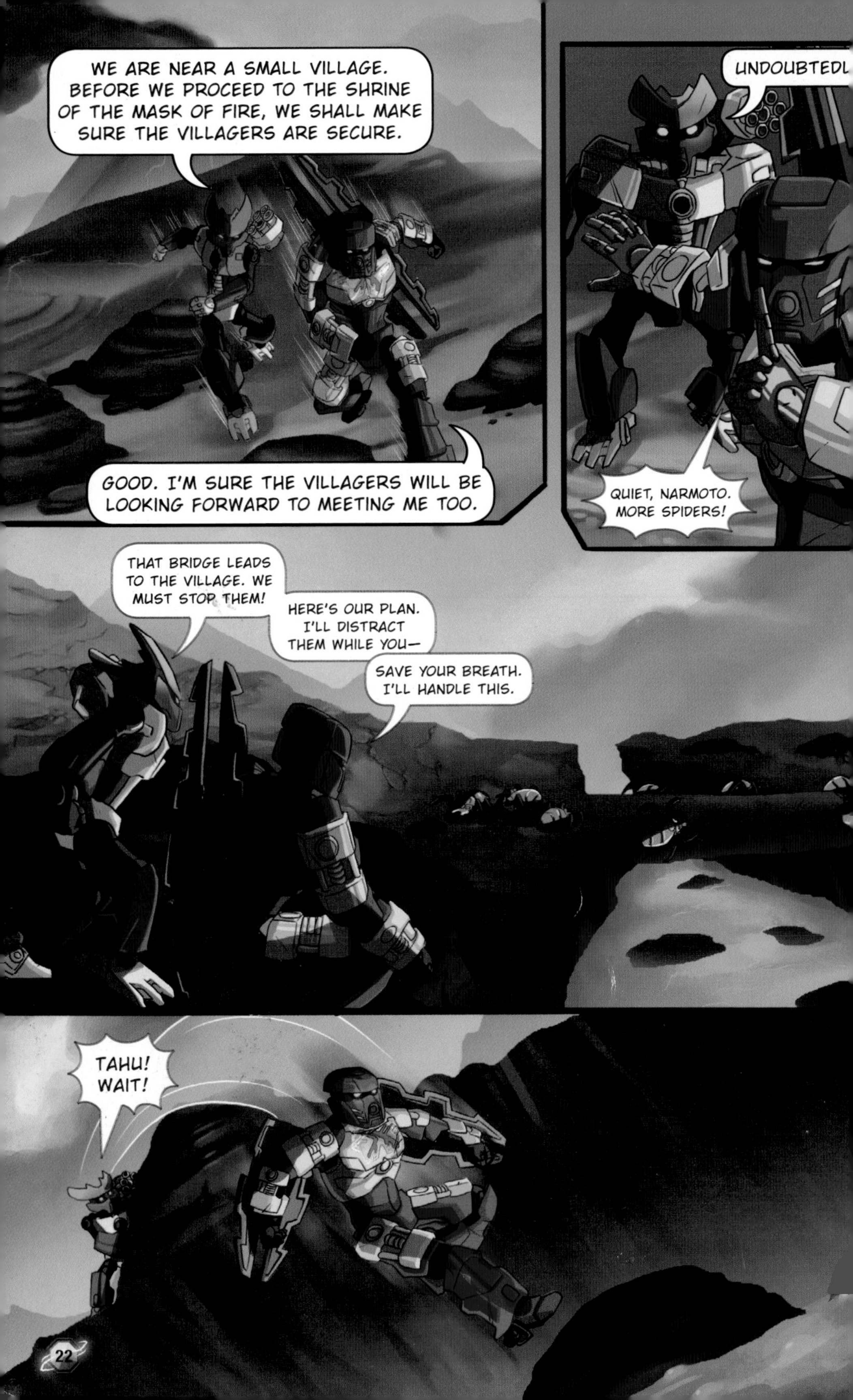
WE ARE NEAR A SMALL VILLAGE. BEFORE WE PROCEED TO THE SHRINE OF THE MASK OF FIRE, WE SHALL MAKE SURE THE VILLAGERS ARE SECURE.
GOOD. I'M SURE THE VILLAGERS WILL BE LOOKING FORWARD TO MEETING ME TOO.
UNDOUBTEDL
QUIET, NARMOTO. MORE SPIDERS!
THAT BRIDGE LEADS TO THE VILLAGE. WE MUST STOP THEM!
HERE'S OUR PLAN. I'LL DISTRACT THEM WHILE YOU—
SAVE YOUR BREATH. I'LL HANDLE THIS.
TAHU! WAIT!

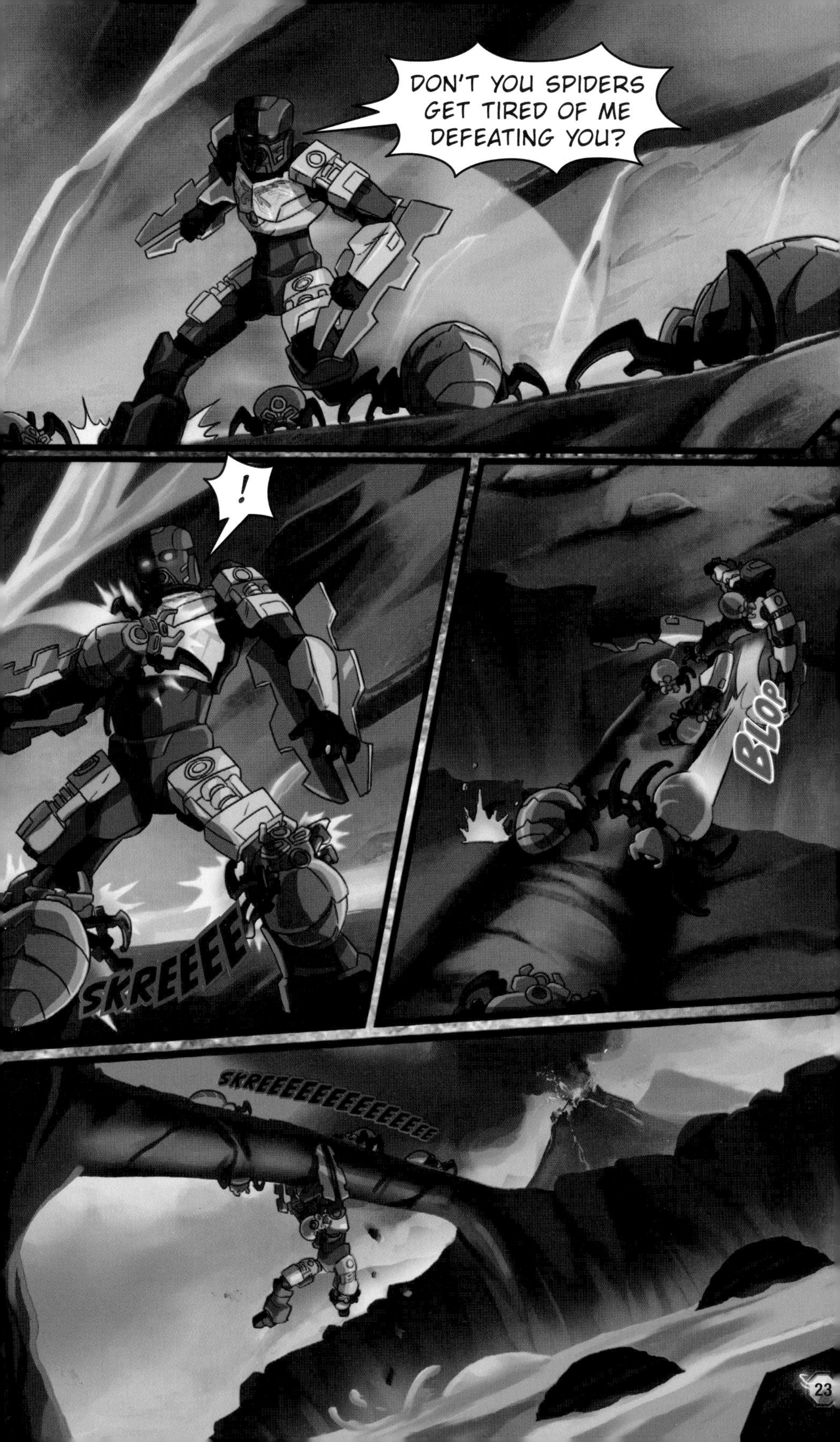
DON'T YOU SPIDERS GET TIRED OF ME DEFEATING YOU?
!
SKREEEEE
BLOP
SKREEEEEEEEEEEEEEEE

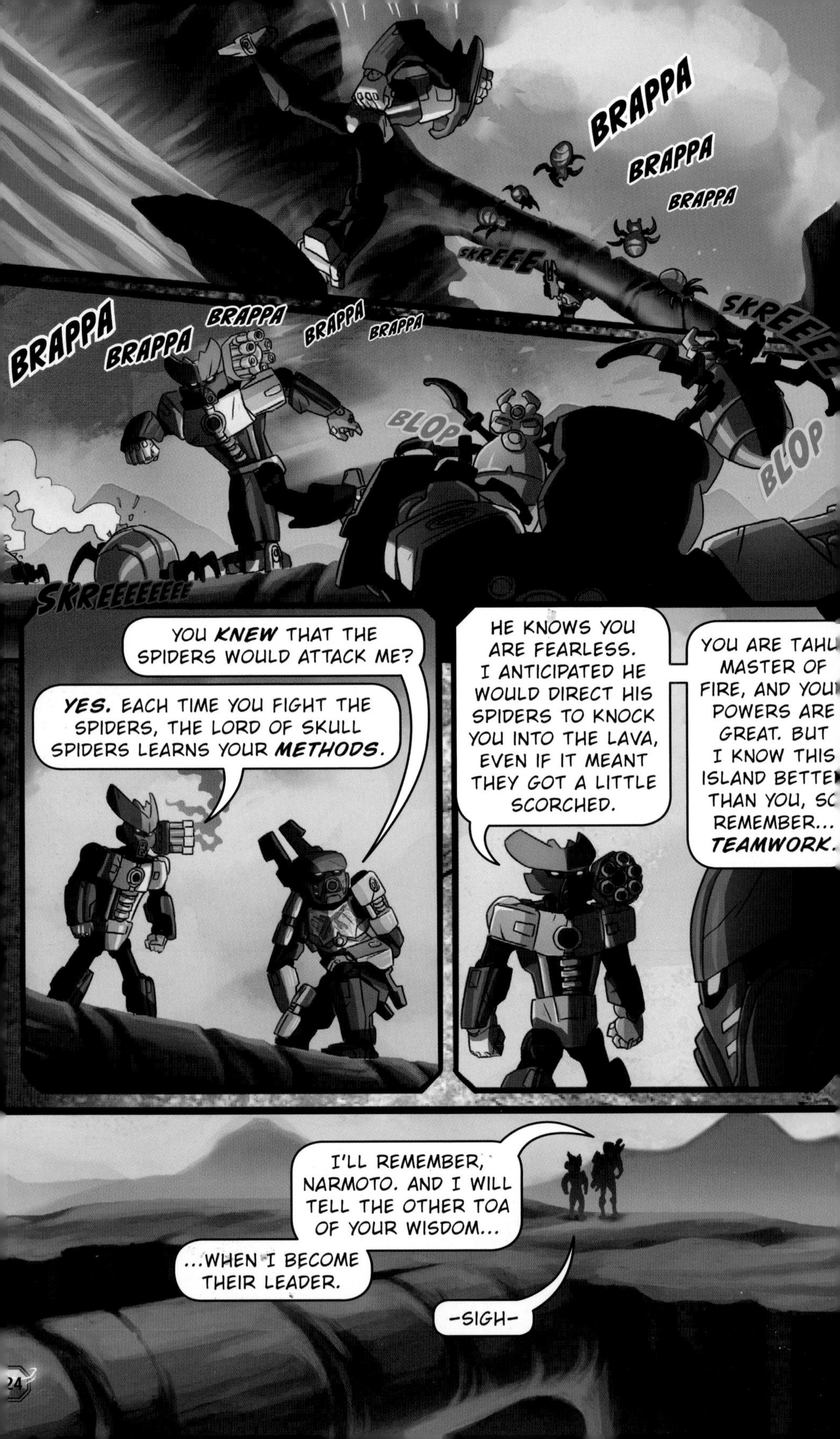
BRAPPA
BRAPPA
BRAPPA
SKREEE
BRAPPA
BRAPPA
BRAPPA
BRAPPA
BRAPPA
SKREEEEE
BLOP
BLOP
SKREEEEEEE
YOU KNEW THAT THE SPIDERS WOULD ATTACK ME?
YES. EACH TIME YOU FIGHT THE SPIDERS, THE LORD OF SKULL SPIDERS LEARNS YOUR METHODS.
HE KNOWS YOU ARE FEARLESS. I ANTICIPATED HE WOULD DIRECT HIS SPIDERS TO KNOCK YOU INTO THE LAVA, EVEN IF IT MEANT THEY GOT A LITTLE SCORCHED.
YOU ARE TAHU MASTER OF FIRE, AND YOUR POWERS ARE GREAT. BUT I KNOW THIS ISLAND BETTER THAN YOU, SO REMEMBER... TEAMWORK.
I'LL REMEMBER, NARMOTO. AND I WILL TELL THE OTHER TOA OF YOUR WISDOM...
...WHEN I BECOME THEIR LEADER.
-SIGH-

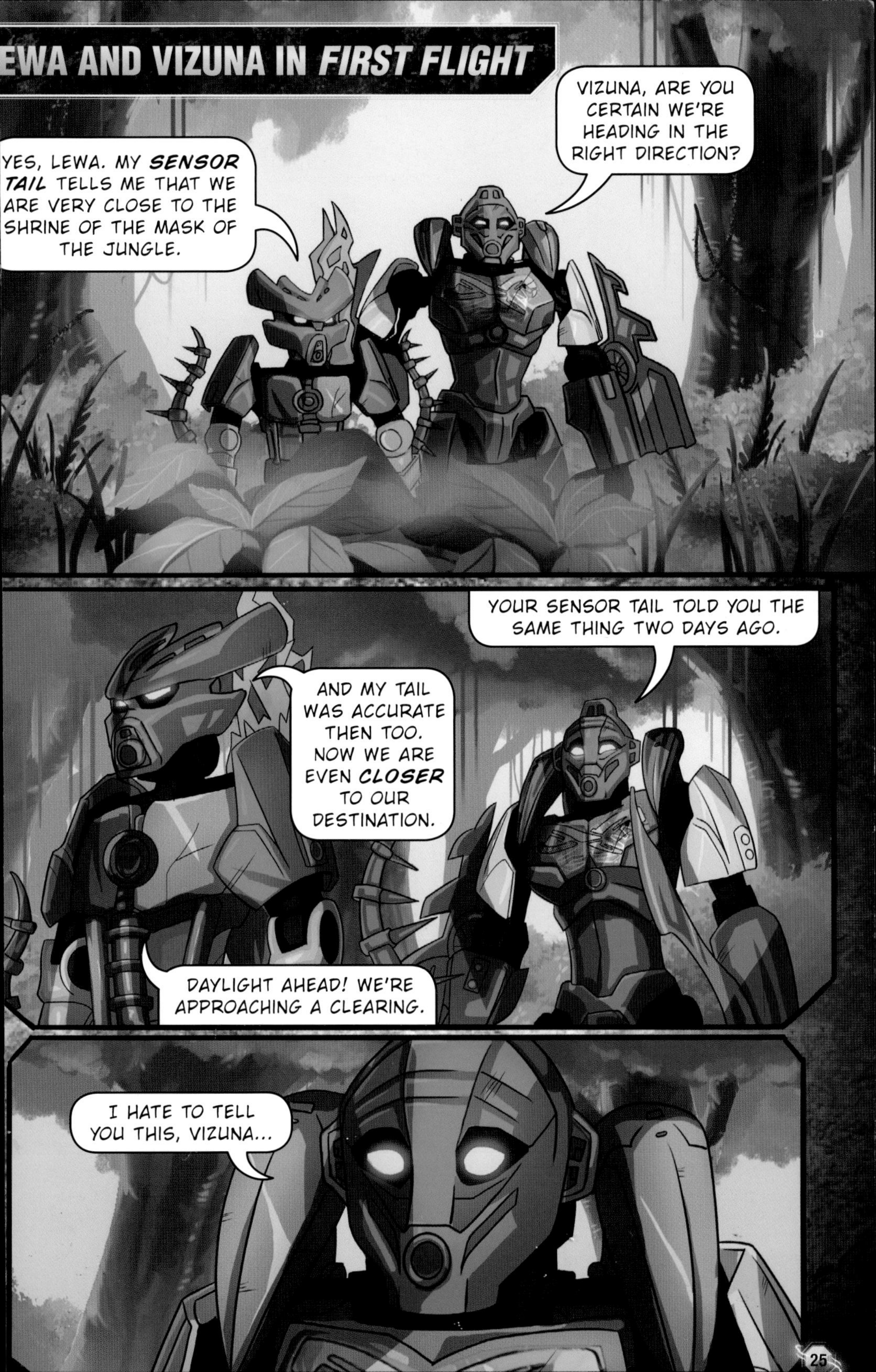
VIZUNA, ARE YOU CERTAIN WE'RE HEADING IN THE RIGHT DIRECTION?
YES, LEWA. MY **SENSOR TAIL** TELLS ME THAT WE ARE VERY CLOSE TO THE SHRINE OF THE MASK OF THE JUNGLE.
YOUR SENSOR TAIL TOLD YOU THE SAME THING TWO DAYS AGO.
AND MY TAIL WAS ACCURATE THEN TOO. NOW WE ARE EVEN **CLOSER** TO OUR DESTINATION.
DAYLIGHT AHEAD! WE'RE APPROACHING A CLEARING.
I HATE TO TELL YOU THIS, VIZUNA...

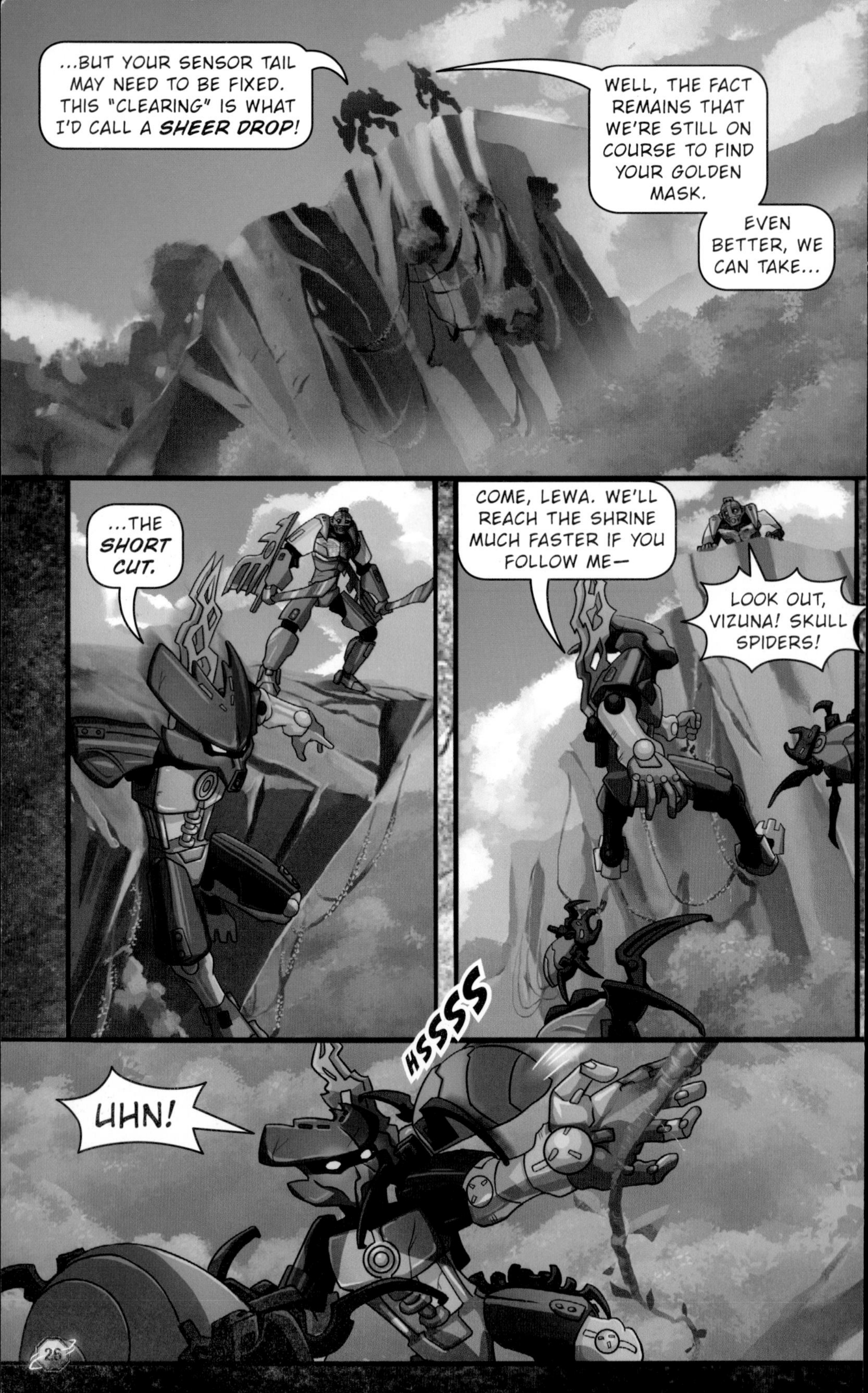
...BUT YOUR SENSOR TAIL MAY NEED TO BE FIXED. THIS "CLEARING" IS WHAT I'D CALL A SHEER DROP!
WELL, THE FACT REMAINS THAT WE'RE STILL ON COURSE TO FIND YOUR GOLDEN MASK.
EVEN BETTER, WE CAN TAKE...
...THE SHORT CUT.
COME, LEWA. WE'LL REACH THE SHRINE MUCH FASTER IF YOU FOLLOW ME—
LOOK OUT, VIZUNA! SKULL SPIDERS!
HSSSSS
UHN!

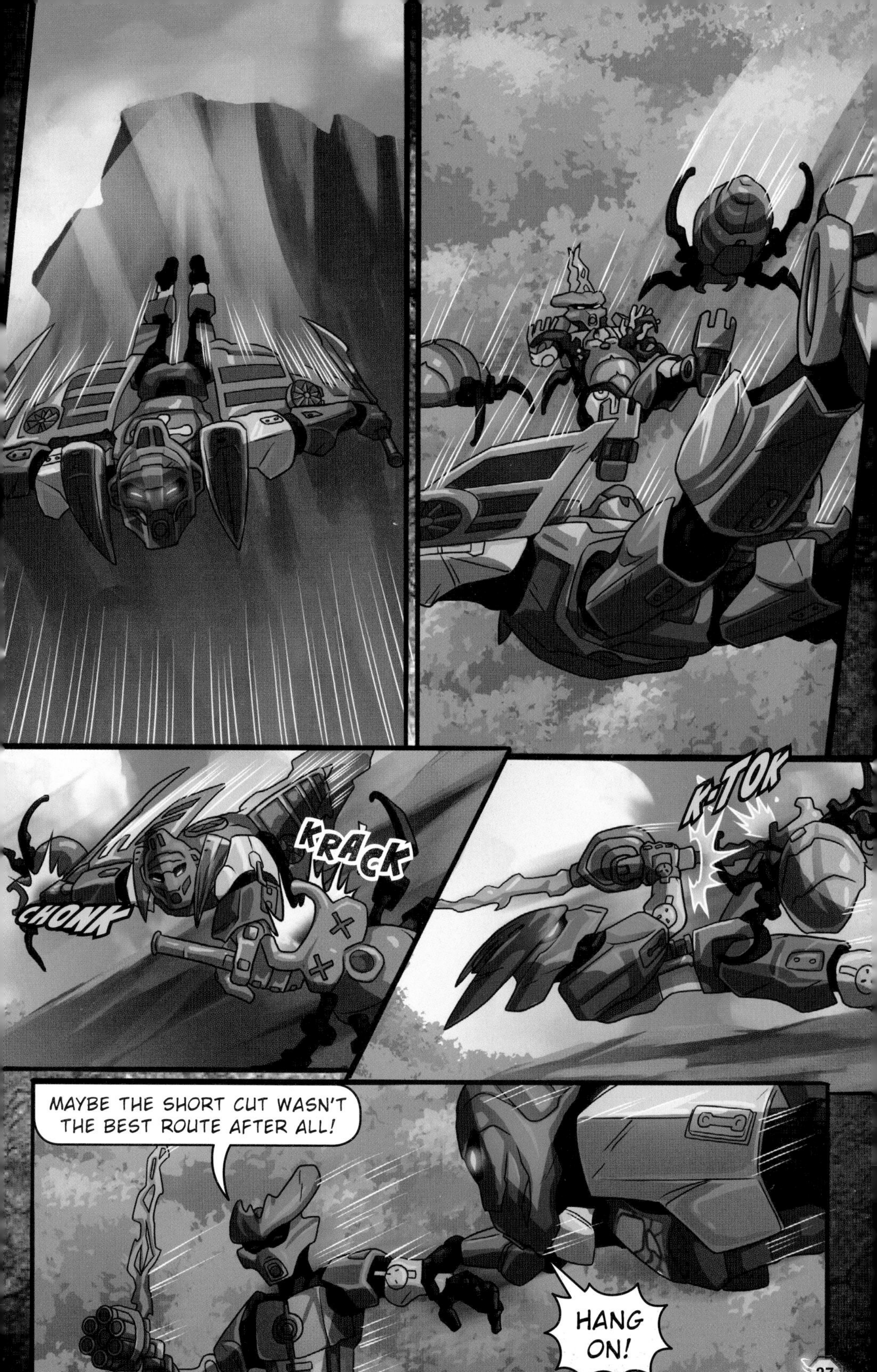
KRACK
CHONK
K-TOK
MAYBE THE SHORT CUT WASN'T THE BEST ROUTE AFTER ALL!
HANG ON!

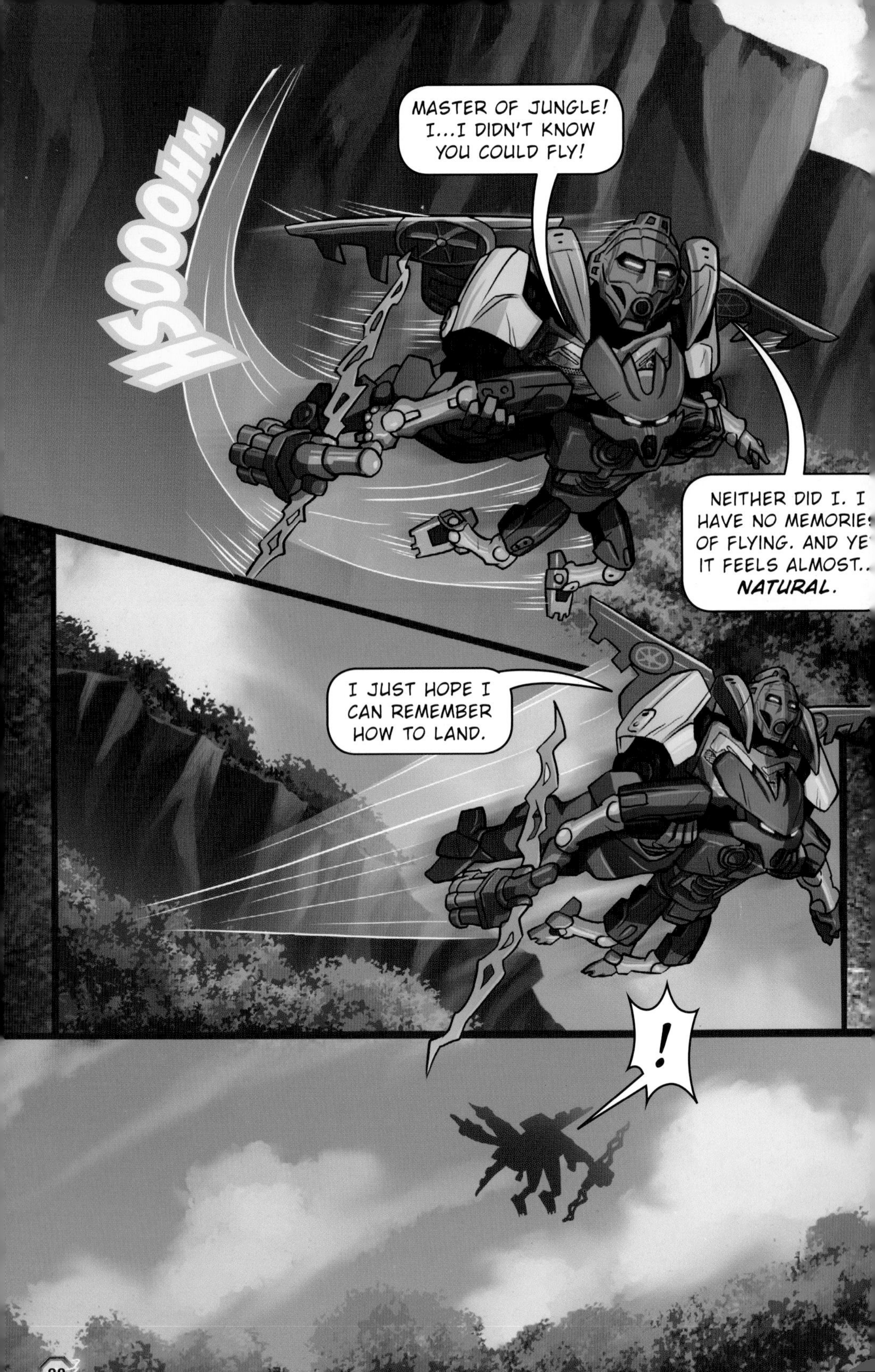
WHOOSH
MASTER OF JUNGLE! I...I DIDN'T KNOW YOU COULD FLY!
NEITHER DID I. I HAVE NO MEMORIES OF FLYING. AND YET IT FEELS ALMOST... NATURAL.
I JUST HOPE I CAN REMEMBER HOW TO LAND.
!

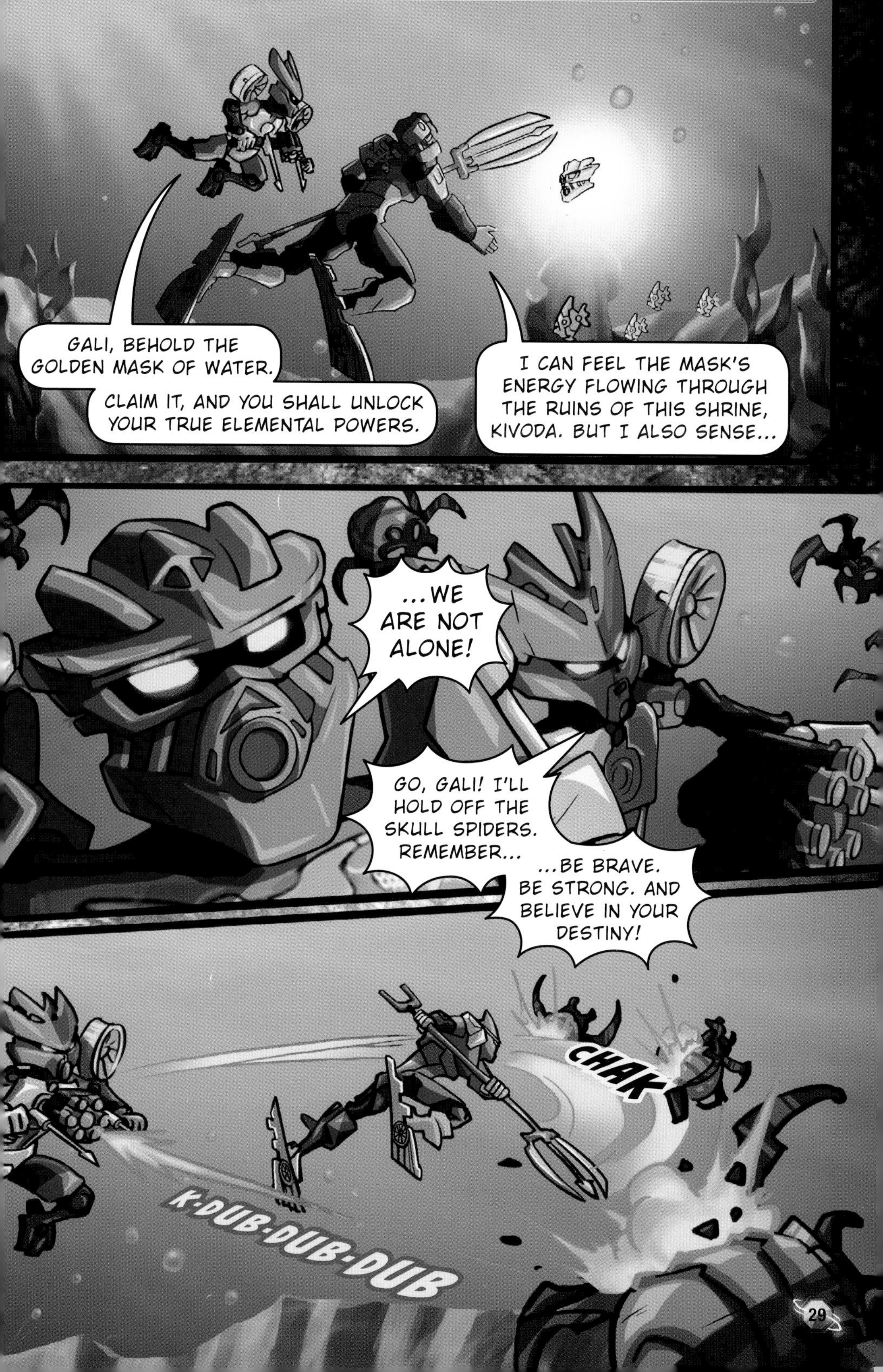
GALI, BEHOLD THE GOLDEN MASK OF WATER.
CLAIM IT, AND YOU SHALL UNLOCK YOUR TRUE ELEMENTAL POWERS.
I CAN FEEL THE MASK'S ENERGY FLOWING THROUGH THE RUINS OF THIS SHRINE, KIVODA. BUT I ALSO SENSE...
...WE ARE NOT ALONE!
GO, GALI! I'LL HOLD OFF THE SKULL SPIDERS. REMEMBER...
...BE BRAVE. BE STRONG. AND BELIEVE IN YOUR DESTINY!
CHAK
K-DUB-DUB-DUB

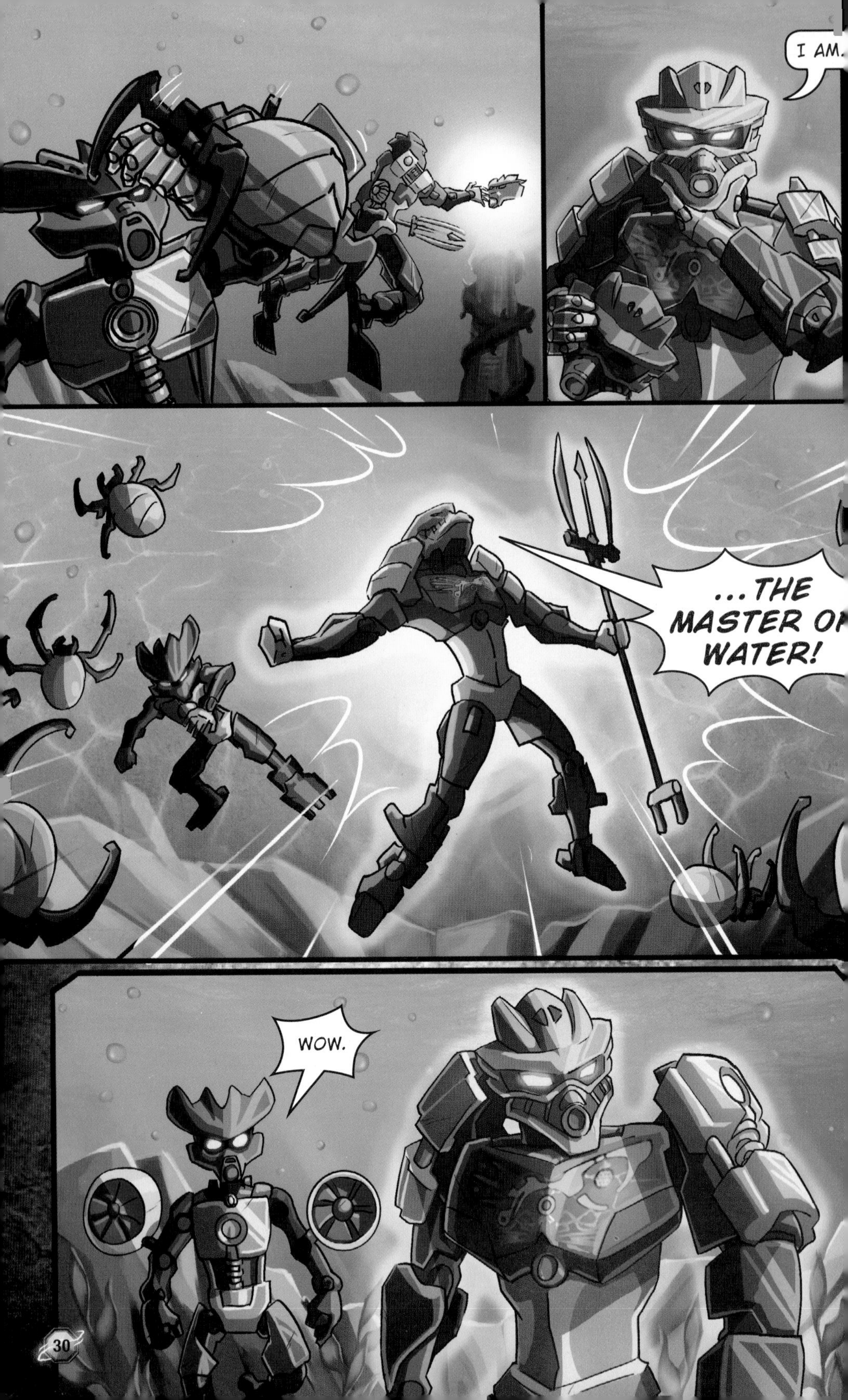

I AM.
...THE MASTER OF WATER!
WOW.

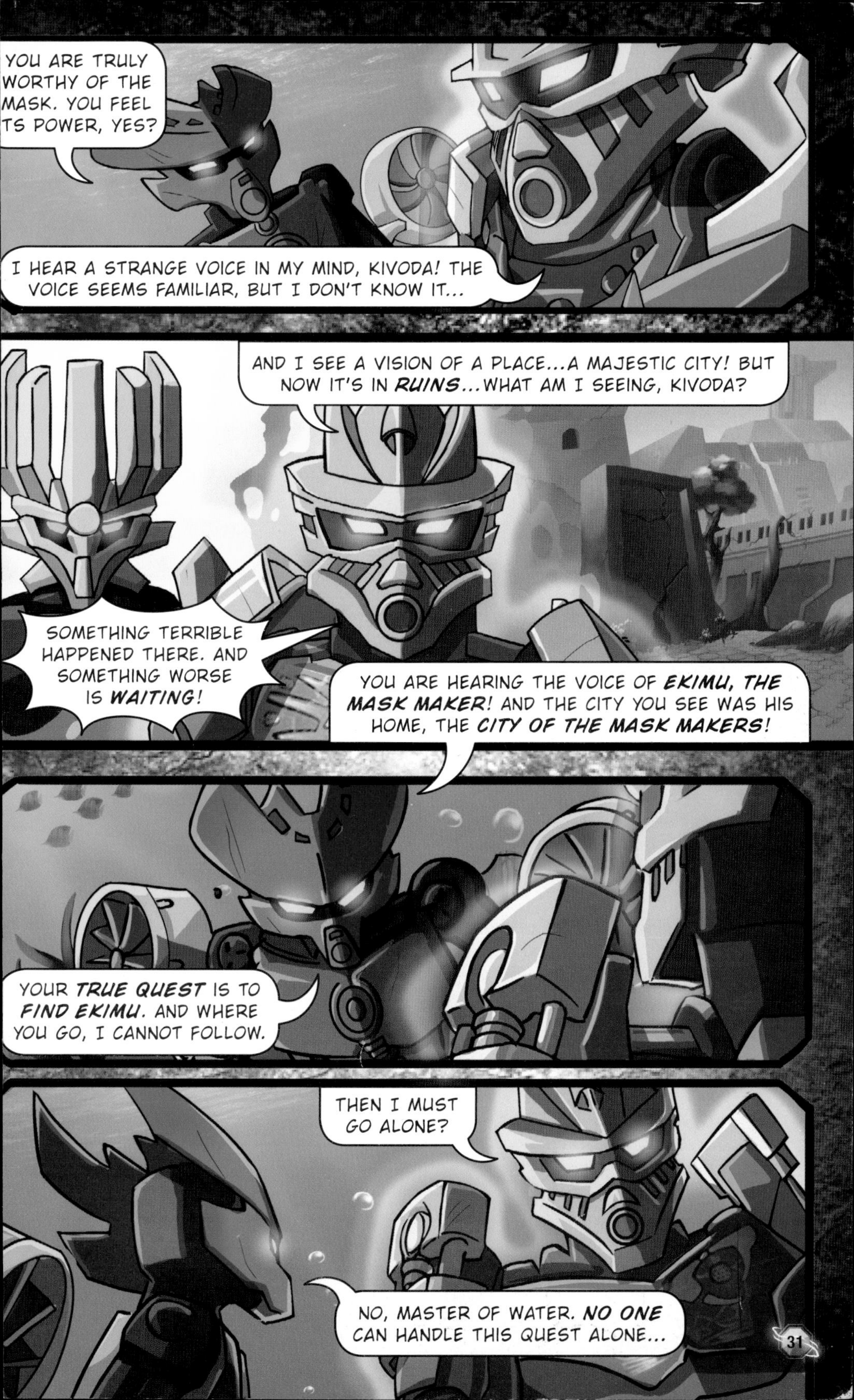
YOU ARE TRULY WORTHY OF THE MASK. YOU FEEL TS POWER, YES?
I HEAR A STRANGE VOICE IN MY MIND, KIVODA! THE VOICE SEEMS FAMILIAR, BUT I DON'T KNOW IT...
AND I SEE A VISION OF A PLACE...A MAJESTIC CITY! BUT NOW IT'S IN RUINS...WHAT AM I SEEING, KIVODA?
SOMETHING TERRIBLE HAPPENED THERE. AND SOMETHING WORSE IS WAITING!
YOU ARE HEARING THE VOICE OF EKIMU, THE MASK MAKER! AND THE CITY YOU SEE WAS HIS HOME, THE CITY OF THE MASK MAKERS!
YOUR TRUE QUEST IS TO FIND EKIMU. AND WHERE YOU GO, I CANNOT FOLLOW.
THEN I MUST GO ALONE?
NO, MASTER OF WATER. NO ONE CAN HANDLE THIS QUEST ALONE...

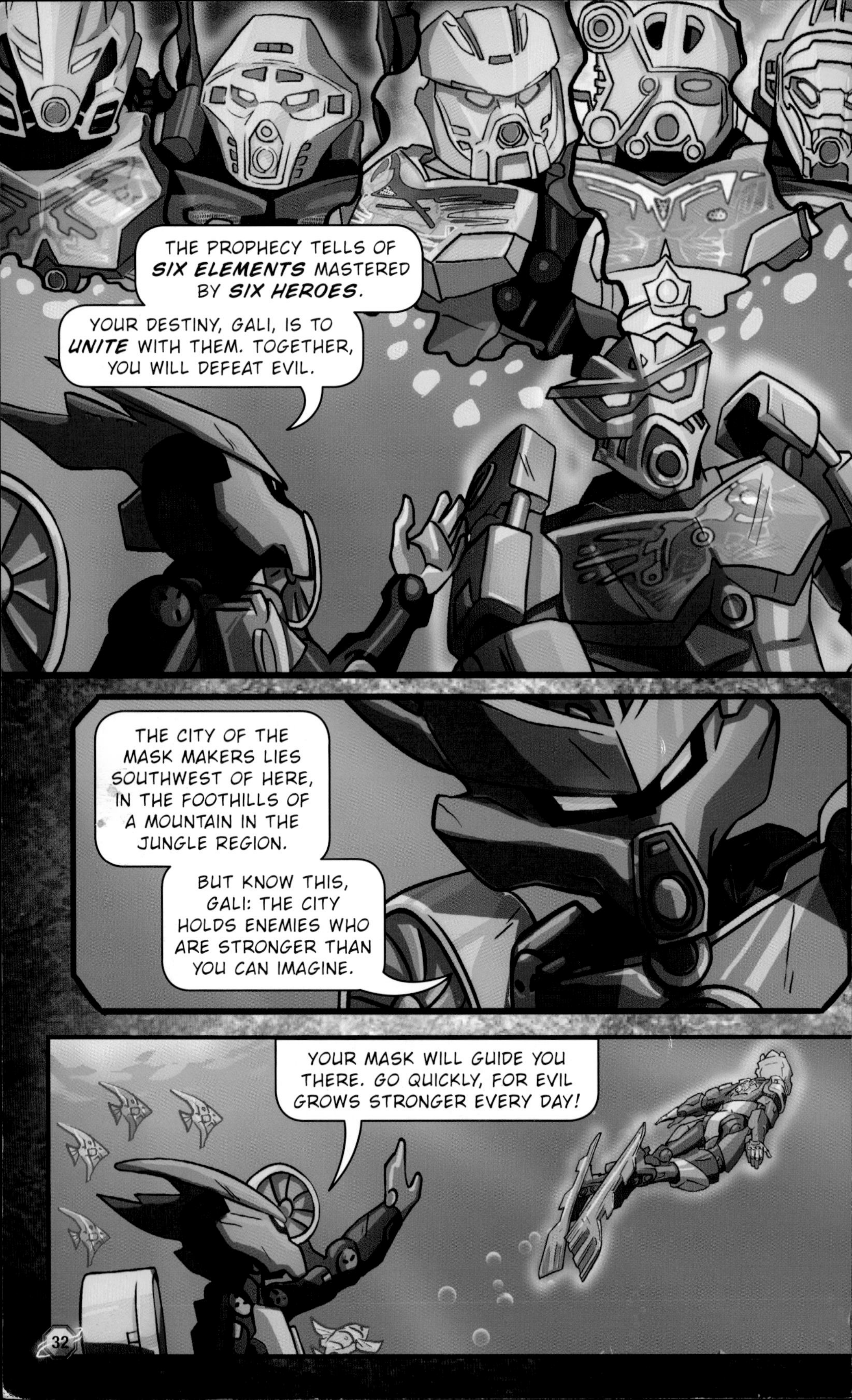
THE PROPHECY TELLS OF SIX ELEMENTS MASTERED BY SIX HEROES.
YOUR DESTINY, GALI, IS TO UNITE WITH THEM. TOGETHER, YOU WILL DEFEAT EVIL.
THE CITY OF THE MASK MAKERS LIES SOUTHWEST OF HERE, IN THE FOOTHILLS OF A MOUNTAIN IN THE JUNGLE REGION.
BUT KNOW THIS, GALI: THE CITY HOLDS ENEMIES WHO ARE STRONGER THAN YOU CAN IMAGINE.
YOUR MASK WILL GUIDE YOU THERE. GO QUICKLY, FOR EVIL GROWS STRONGER EVERY DAY!

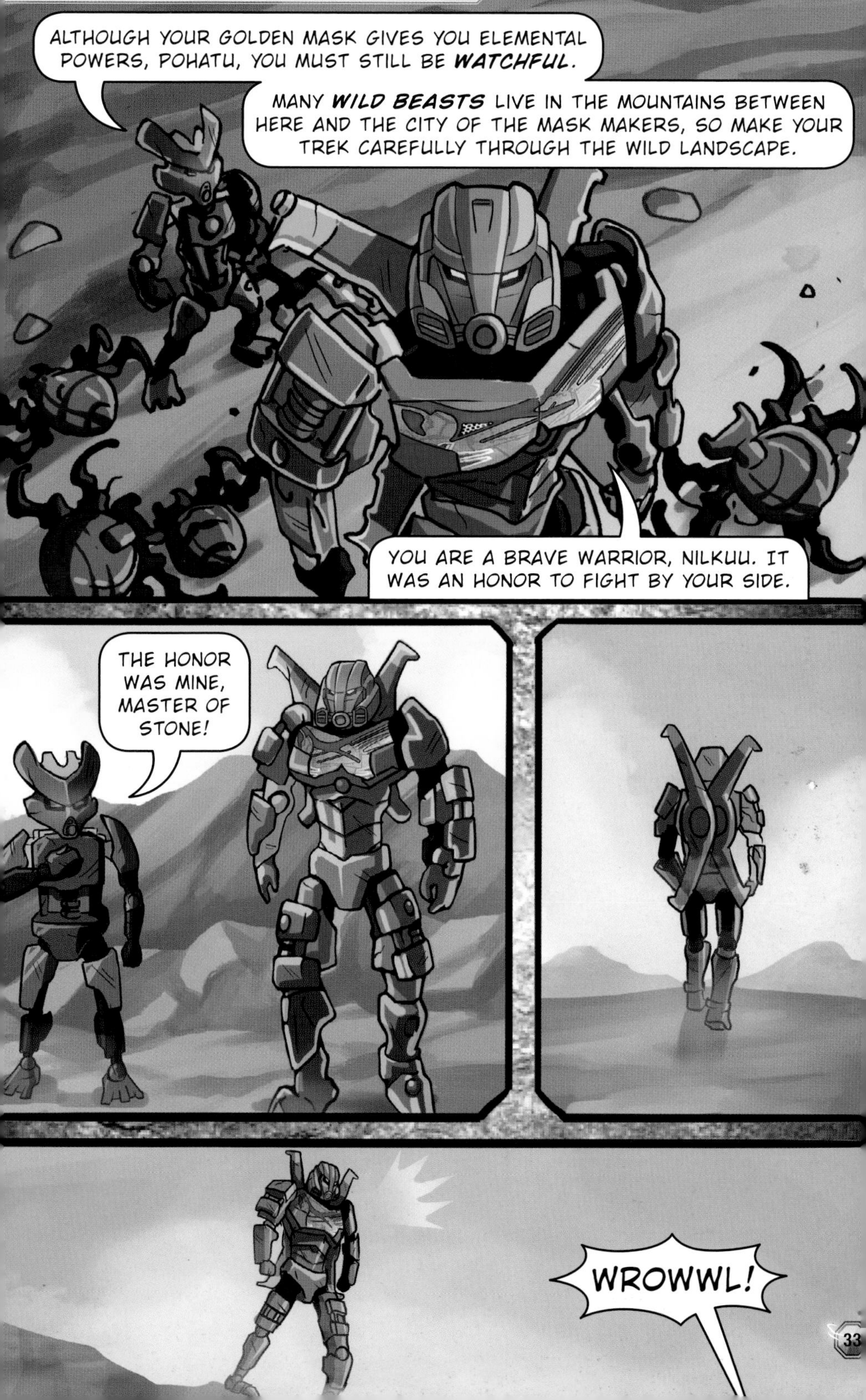
ALTHOUGH YOUR GOLDEN MASK GIVES YOU ELEMENTAL POWERS, POHATU, YOU MUST STILL BE WATCHFUL.
MANY WILD BEASTS LIVE IN THE MOUNTAINS BETWEEN HERE AND THE CITY OF THE MASK MAKERS, SO MAKE YOUR TREK CAREFULLY THROUGH THE WILD LANDSCAPE.
YOU ARE A BRAVE WARRIOR, NILKUU. IT WAS AN HONOR TO FIGHT BY YOUR SIDE.
THE HONOR WAS MINE, MASTER OF STONE!
WROWWL!

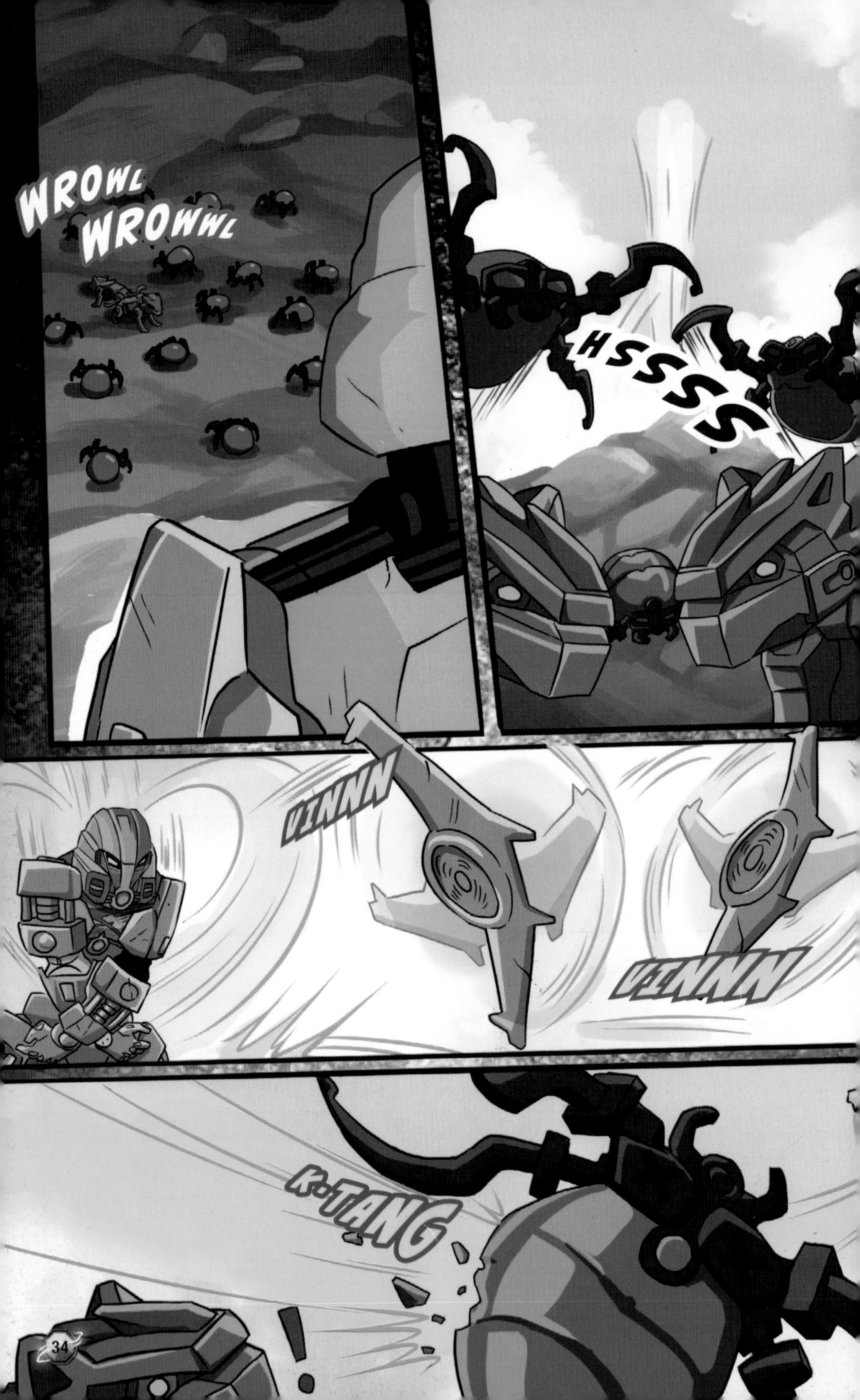
WROWL
WROWWL
HSSSSS
VINNN
VINNN
K-TANG
!

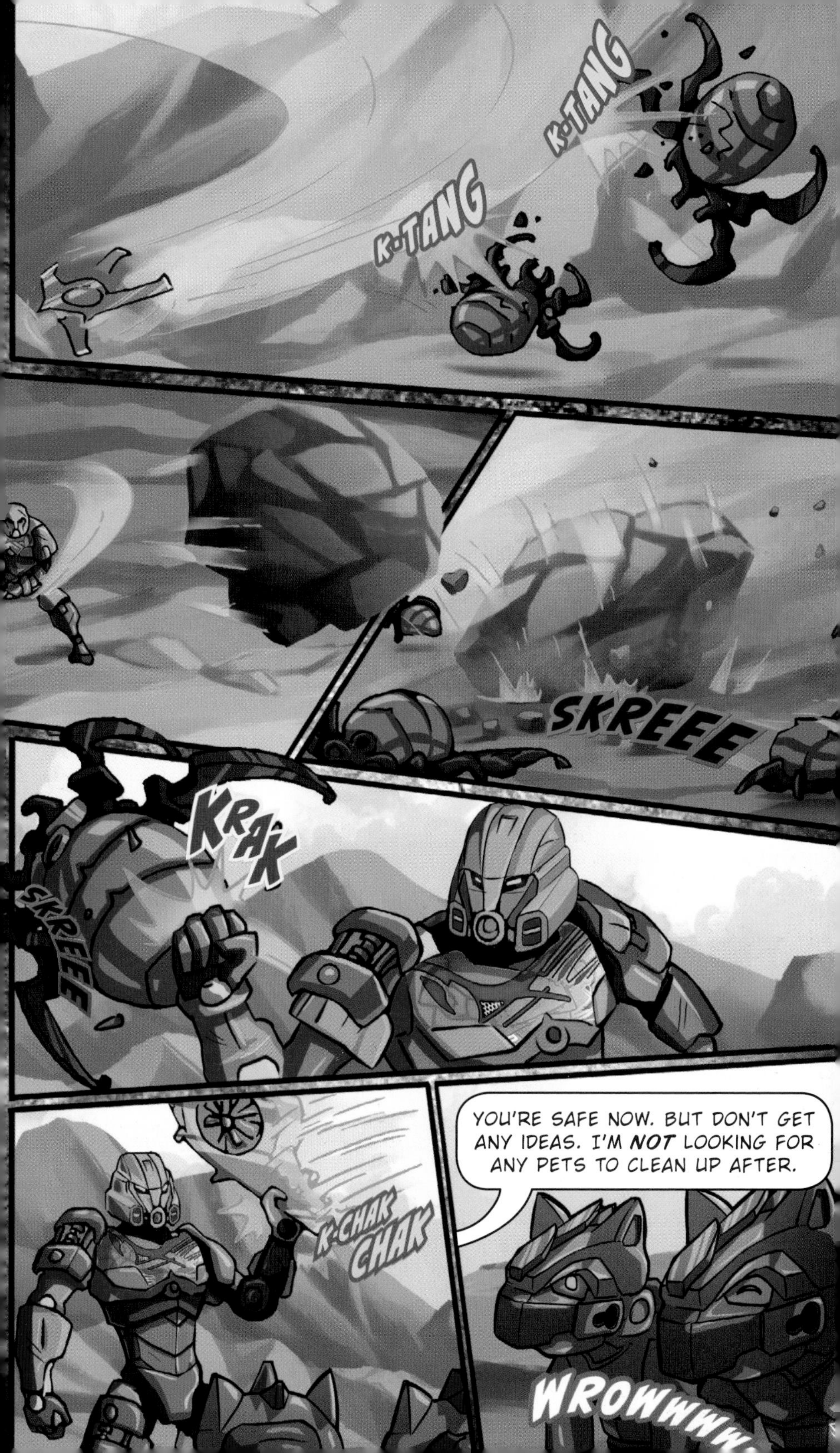
K-TANG
K-TANG
K-TANG
SKREEE
KRAK
SKREEE
K-CHAK
CHAK
YOU'RE SAFE NOW. BUT DON'T GET ANY IDEAS. I'M ***NOT*** LOOKING FOR ANY PETS TO CLEAN UP AFTER.
WROWWWW

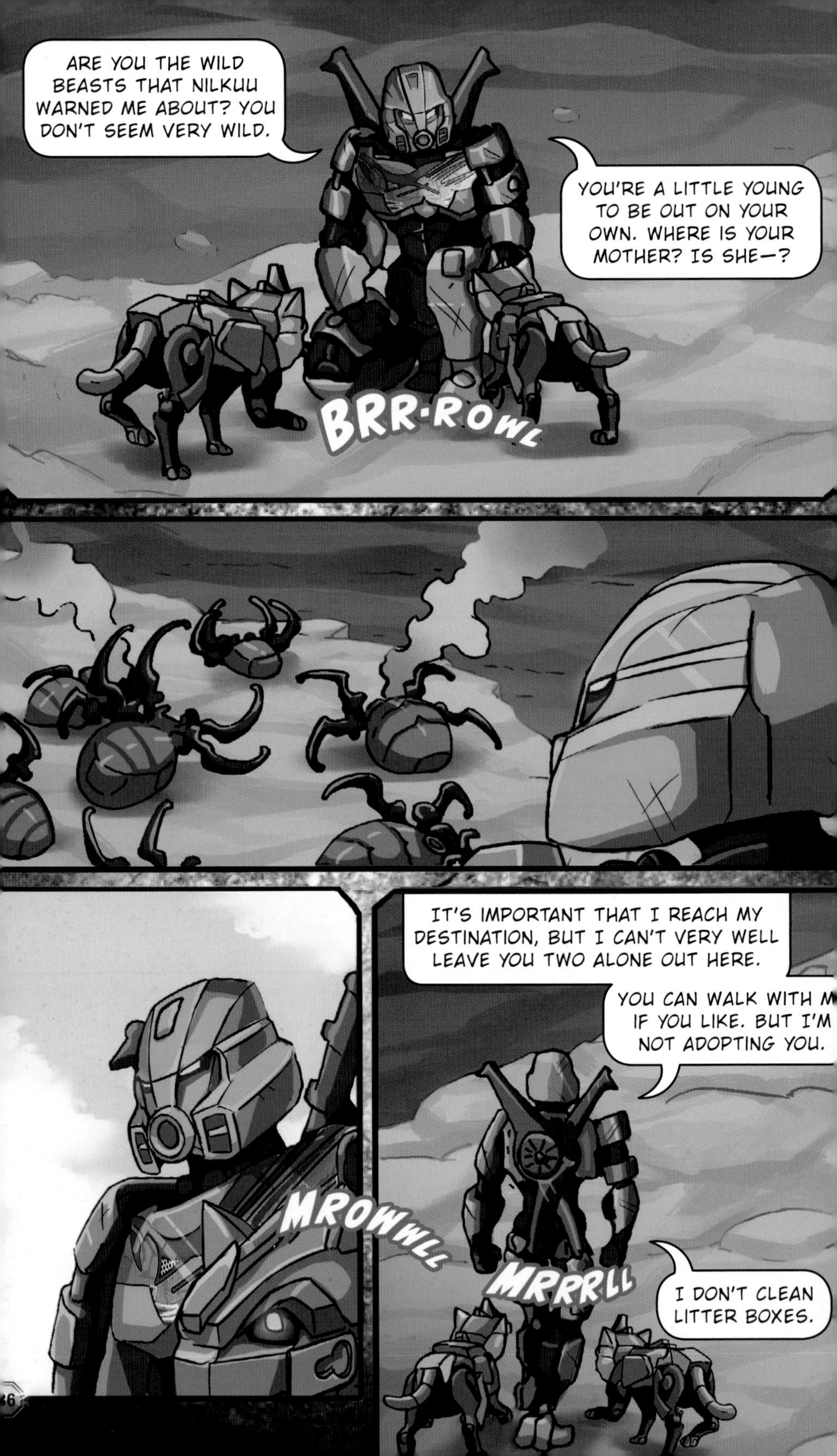
ARE YOU THE WILD BEASTS THAT NILKUU WARNED ME ABOUT? YOU DON'T SEEM VERY WILD.
YOU'RE A LITTLE YOUNG TO BE OUT ON YOUR OWN. WHERE IS YOUR MOTHER? IS SHE—?
BRR-ROWL
IT'S IMPORTANT THAT I REACH MY DESTINATION, BUT I CAN'T VERY WELL LEAVE YOU TWO ALONE OUT HERE.
YOU CAN WALK WITH M
IF YOU LIKE. BUT I'M NOT ADOPTING YOU.
MROWWLL
MRRRLL
I DON'T CLEAN LITTER BOXES.

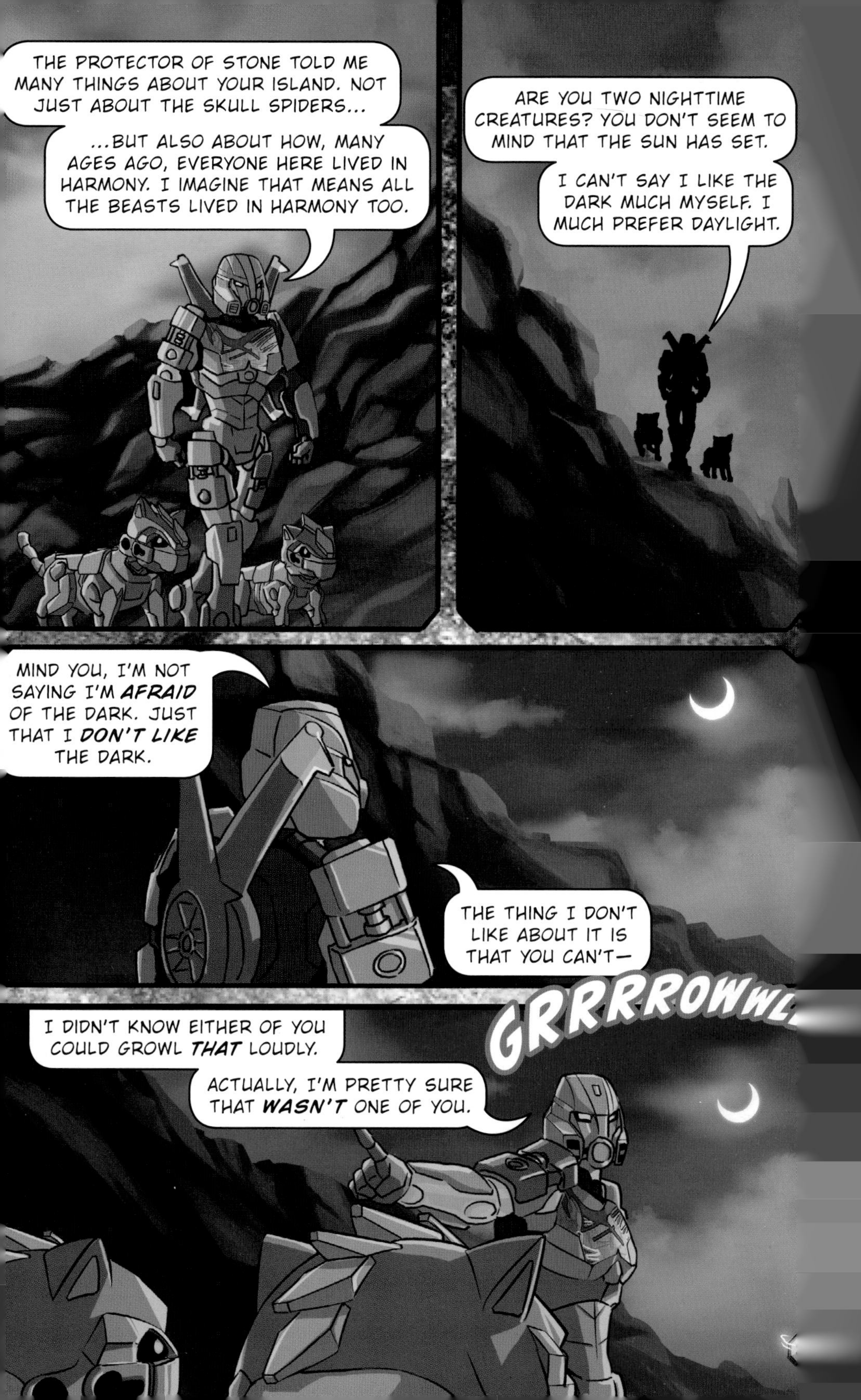
THE PROTECTOR OF STONE TOLD ME MANY THINGS ABOUT YOUR ISLAND. NOT JUST ABOUT THE SKULL SPIDERS...
...BUT ALSO ABOUT HOW, MANY AGES AGO, EVERYONE HERE LIVED IN HARMONY. I IMAGINE THAT MEANS ALL THE BEASTS LIVED IN HARMONY TOO.
ARE YOU TWO NIGHTTIME CREATURES? YOU DON'T SEEM TO MIND THAT THE SUN HAS SET.
I CAN'T SAY I LIKE THE DARK MUCH MYSELF. I MUCH PREFER DAYLIGHT.
MIND YOU, I'M NOT SAYING I'M *AFRAID* OF THE DARK. JUST THAT I *DON'T LIKE* THE DARK.
THE THING I DON'T LIKE ABOUT IT IS THAT YOU CAN'T—
GRRRROWWL
I DIDN'T KNOW EITHER OF YOU COULD GROWL *THAT* LOUDLY.
ACTUALLY, I'M PRETTY SURE THAT *WASN'T* ONE OF YOU.

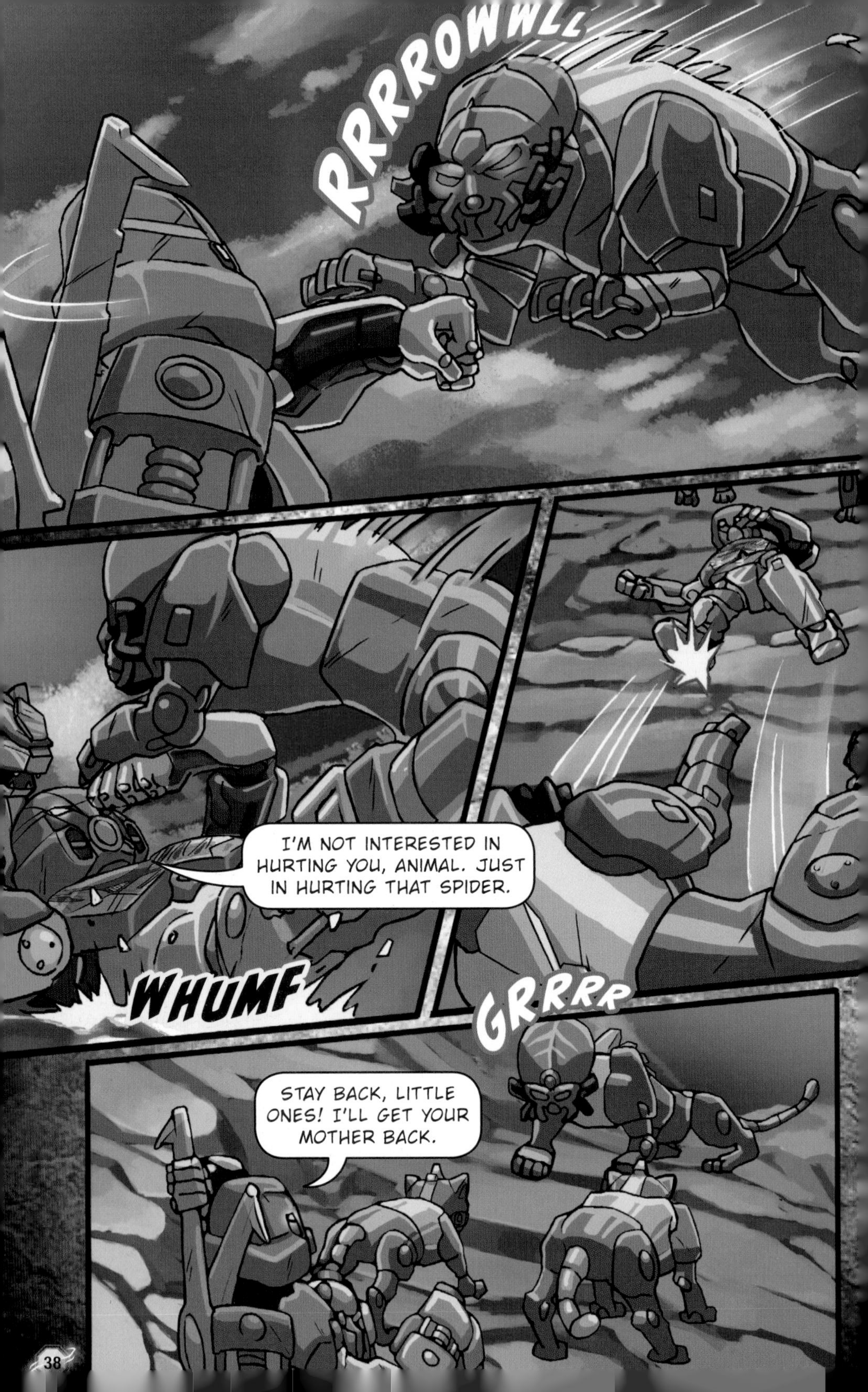
RRRROWWLL
I'M NOT INTERESTED IN HURTING YOU, ANIMAL. JUST IN HURTING THAT SPIDER.
WHUMF
GRRRR
STAY BACK, LITTLE ONES! I'LL GET YOUR MOTHER BACK.

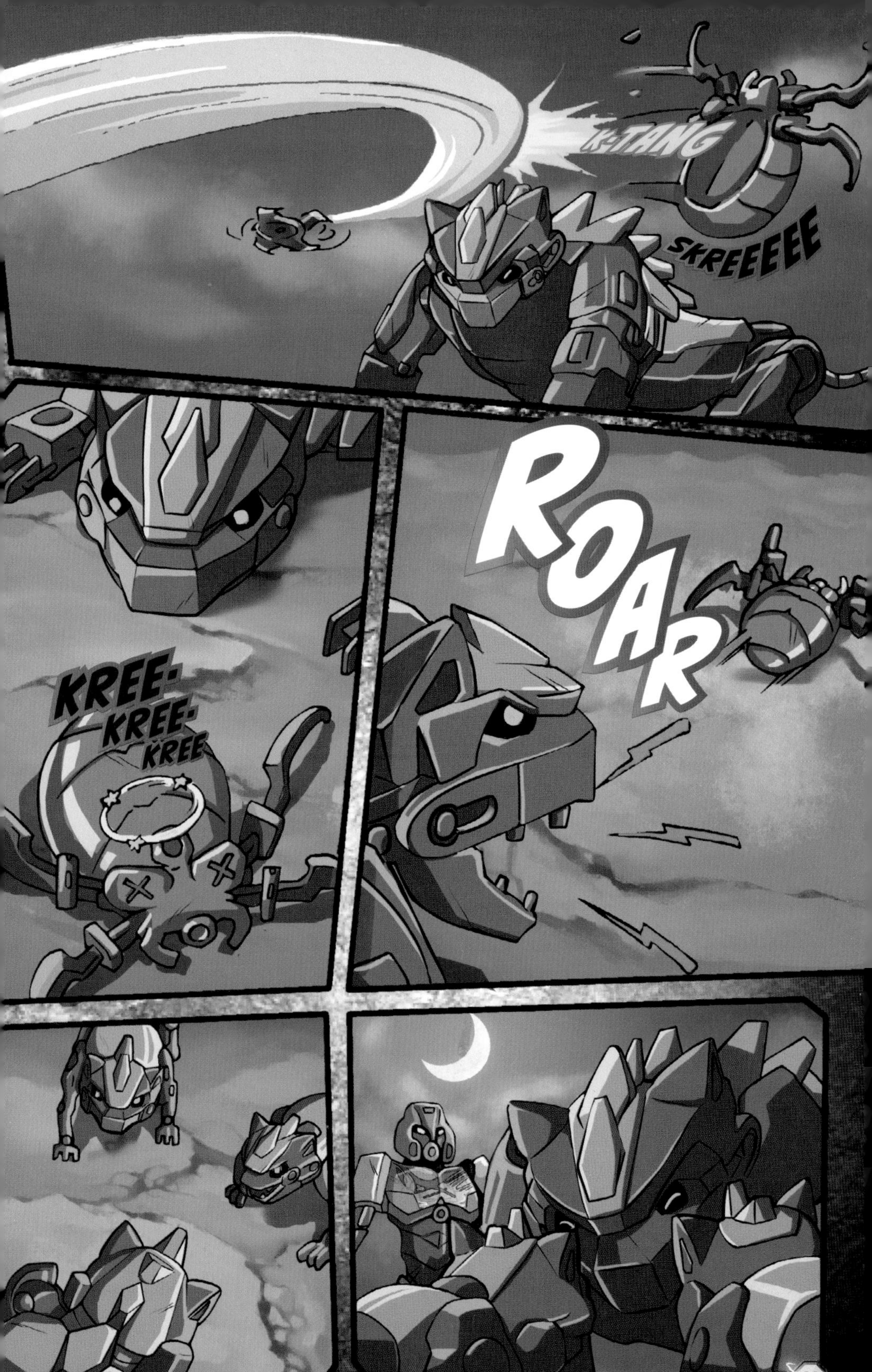
K-TANG
SKREEEEEE
ROAR
KREE-
KREE-
KREE

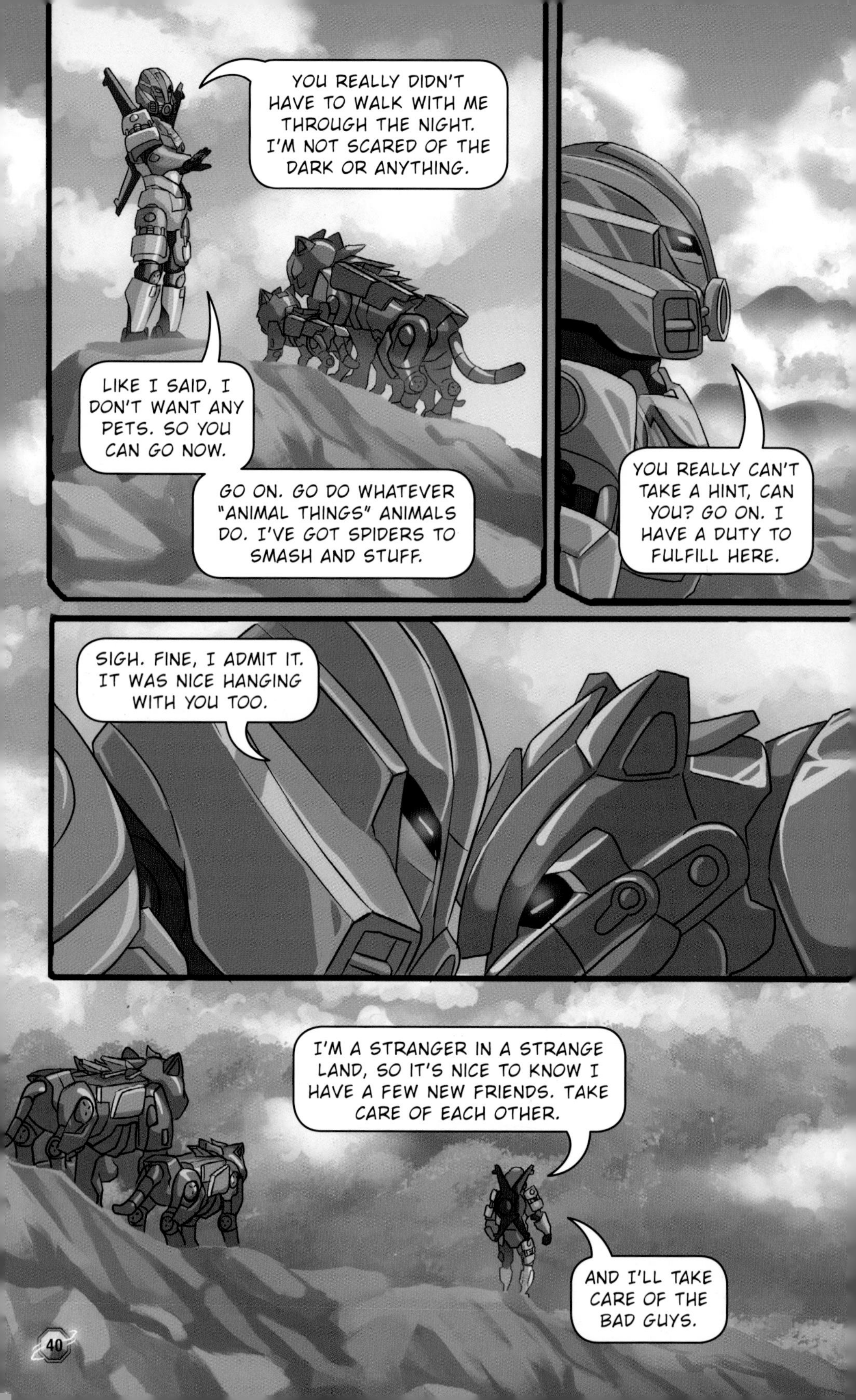
YOU REALLY DIDN'T HAVE TO WALK WITH ME THROUGH THE NIGHT. I'M NOT SCARED OF THE DARK OR ANYTHING.
LIKE I SAID, I DON'T WANT ANY PETS. SO YOU CAN GO NOW.
GO ON. GO DO WHATEVER "ANIMAL THINGS" ANIMALS DO. I'VE GOT SPIDERS TO SMASH AND STUFF.
YOU REALLY CAN'T TAKE A HINT, CAN YOU? GO ON. I HAVE A DUTY TO FULFILL HERE.
SIGH. FINE, I ADMIT IT. IT WAS NICE HANGING WITH YOU TOO.
I'M A STRANGER IN A STRANGE LAND, SO IT'S NICE TO KNOW I HAVE A FEW NEW FRIENDS. TAKE CARE OF EACH OTHER.
AND I'LL TAKE CARE OF THE BAD GUYS.

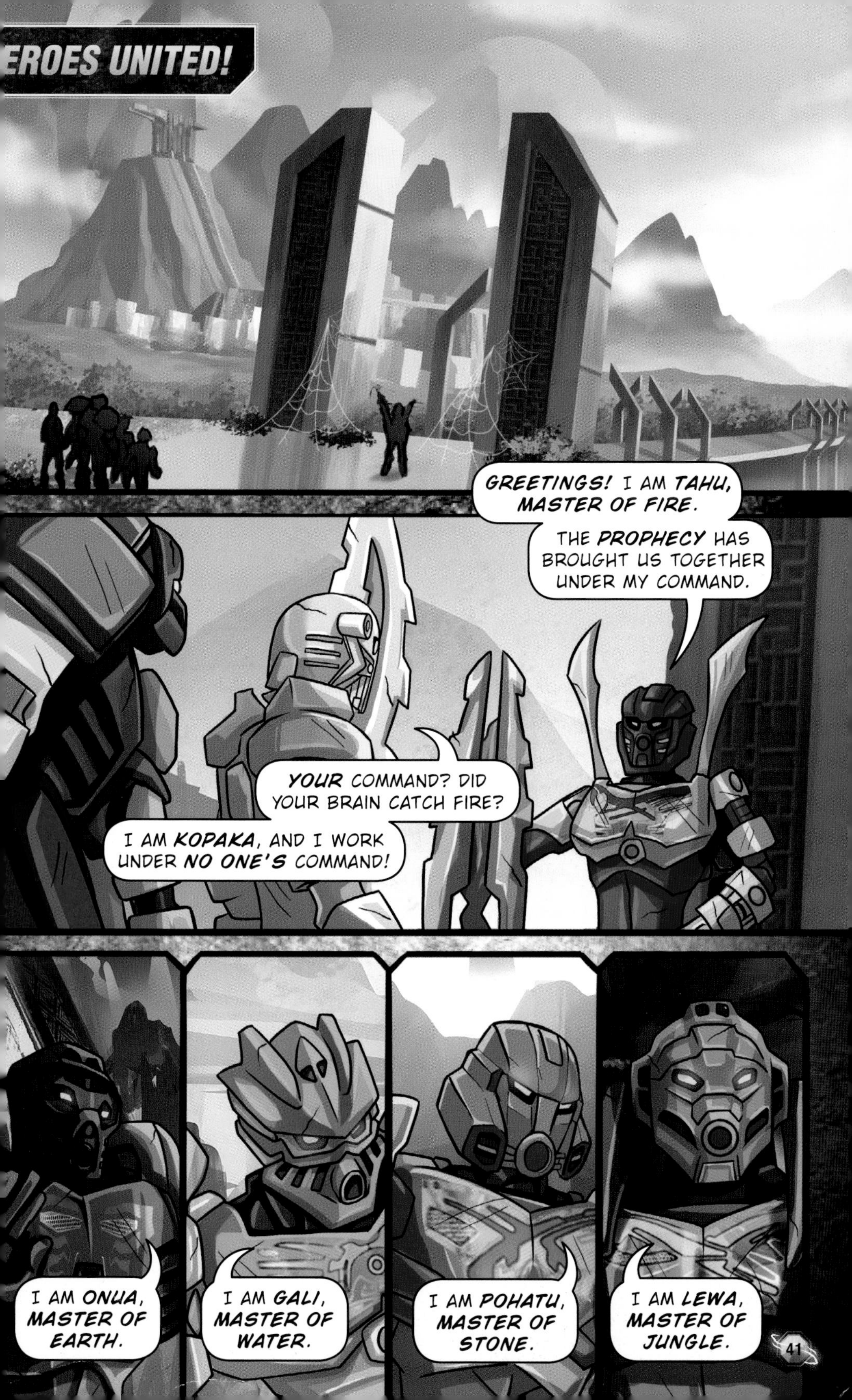
EROES UNITED!
GREETINGS! I AM TAHU, MASTER OF FIRE.
THE PROPHECY HAS BROUGHT US TOGETHER UNDER MY COMMAND.
YOUR COMMAND? DID YOUR BRAIN CATCH FIRE?
I AM KOPAKA, AND I WORK UNDER NO ONE'S COMMAND!
I AM ONUA, MASTER OF EARTH.
I AM GALI, MASTER OF WATER.
I AM POHATU, MASTER OF STONE.
I AM LEWA, MASTER OF JUNGLE.

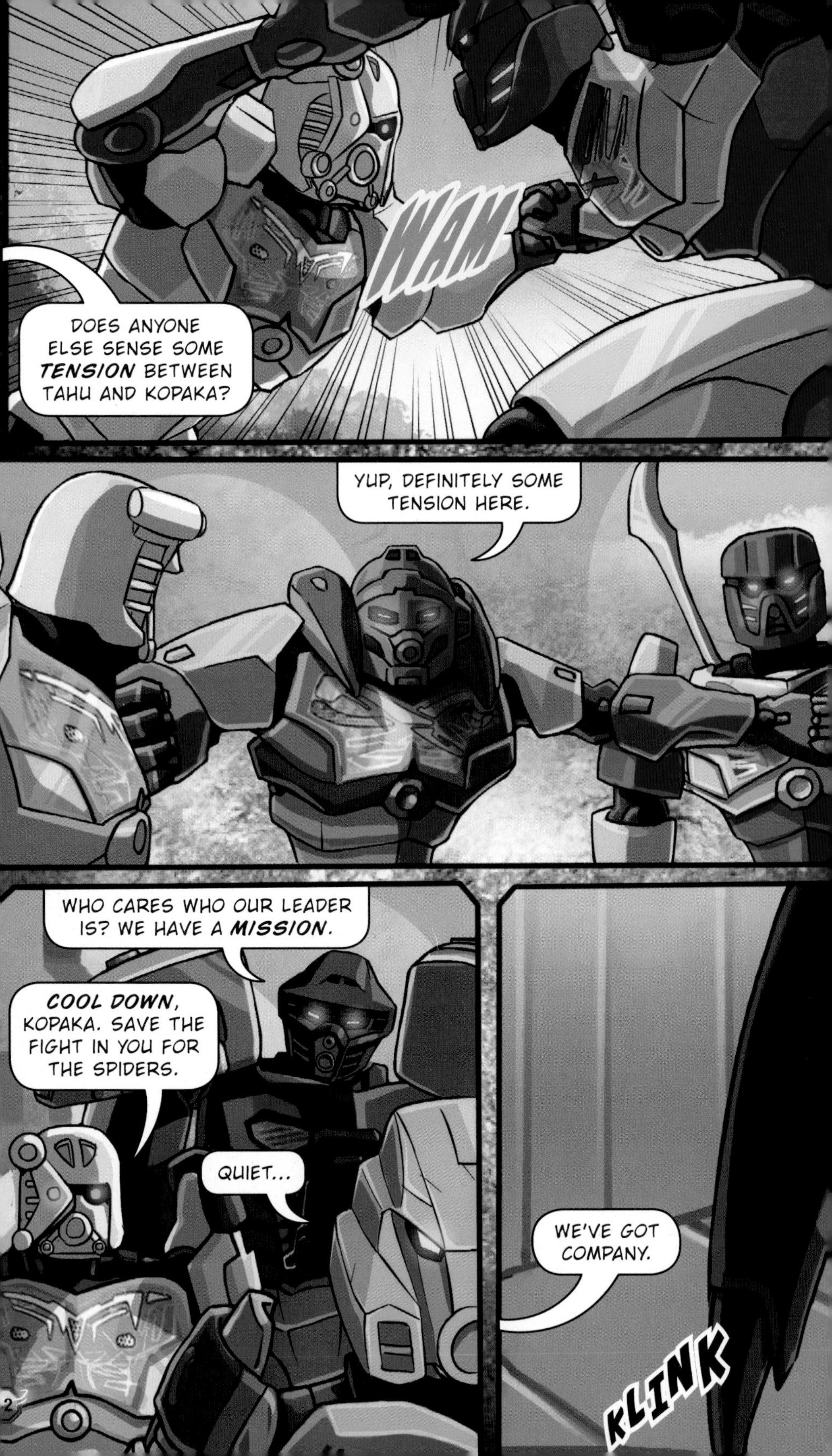
WAM
DOES ANYONE ELSE SENSE SOME TENSION BETWEEN TAHU AND KOPAKA?
YUP, DEFINITELY SOME TENSION HERE.
WHO CARES WHO OUR LEADER IS? WE HAVE A MISSION.
COOL DOWN, KOPAKA. SAVE THE FIGHT IN YOU FOR THE SPIDERS.
QUIET...
WE'VE GOT COMPANY.
KLINK

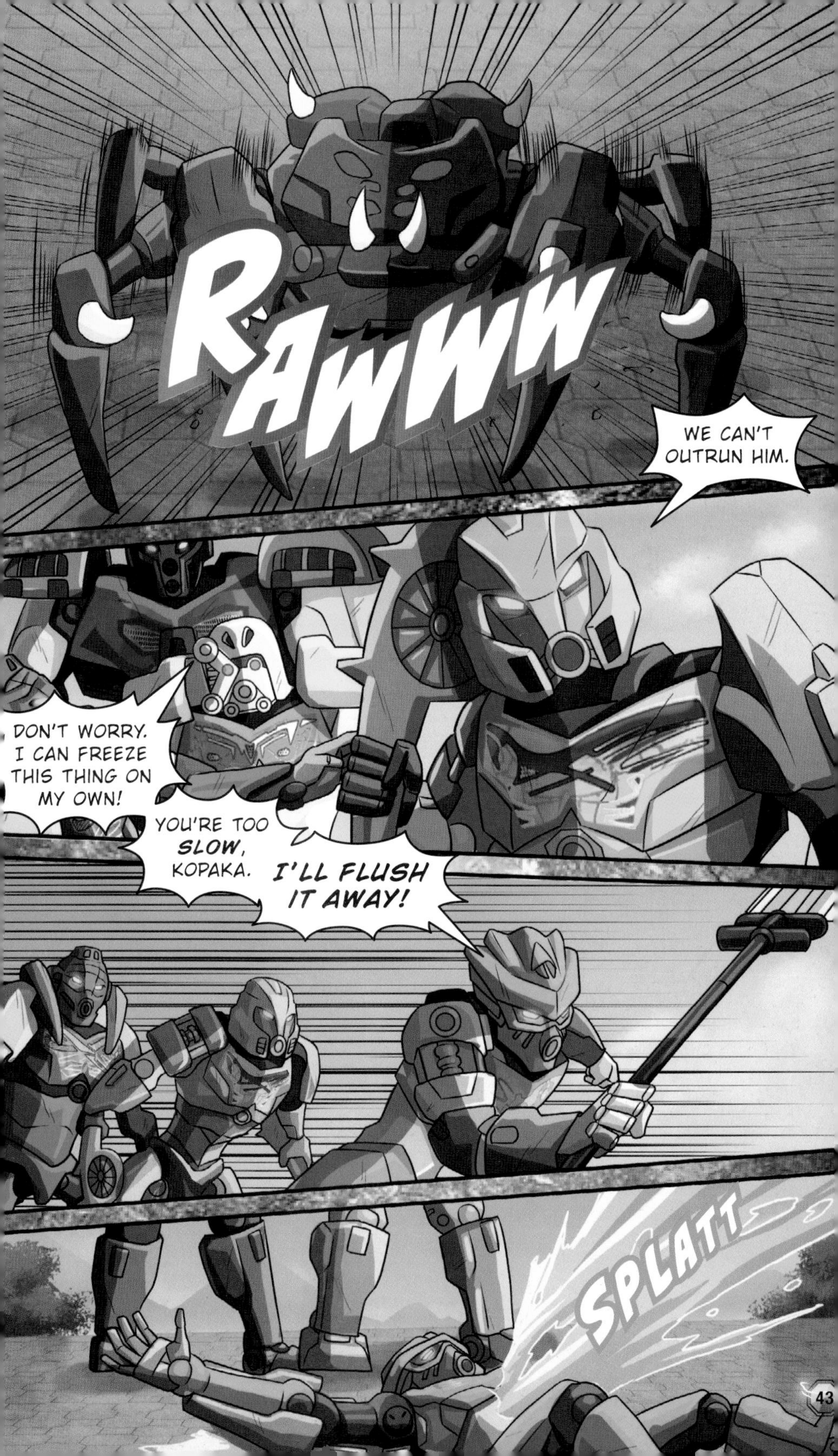

RAWWW
WE CAN'T OUTRUN HIM.
DON'T WORRY. I CAN FREEZE THIS THING ON MY OWN!
YOU'RE TOO SLOW, KOPAKA.
I'LL FLUSH IT AWAY!
SPLATT

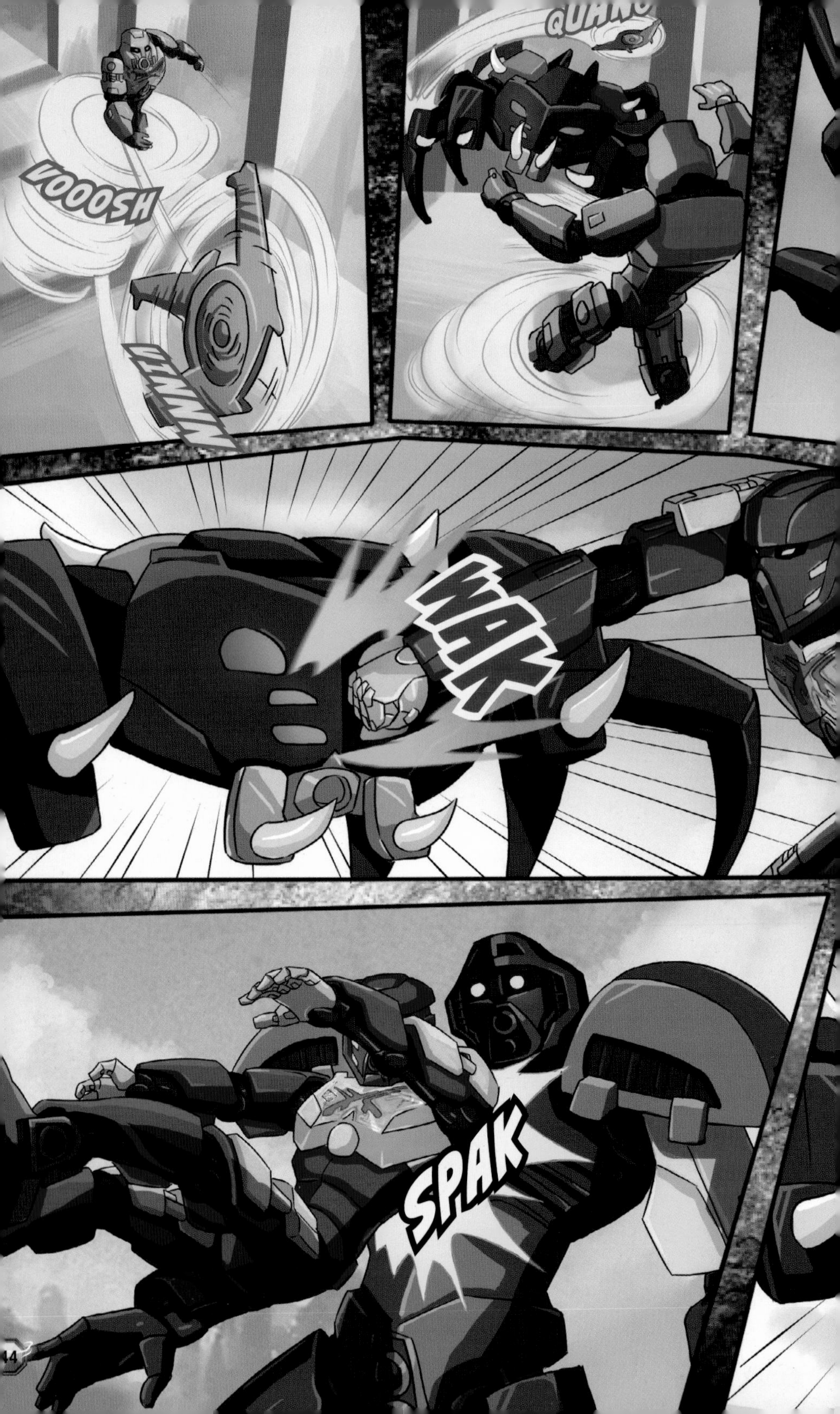
VOOOSH
WAK
SPAK

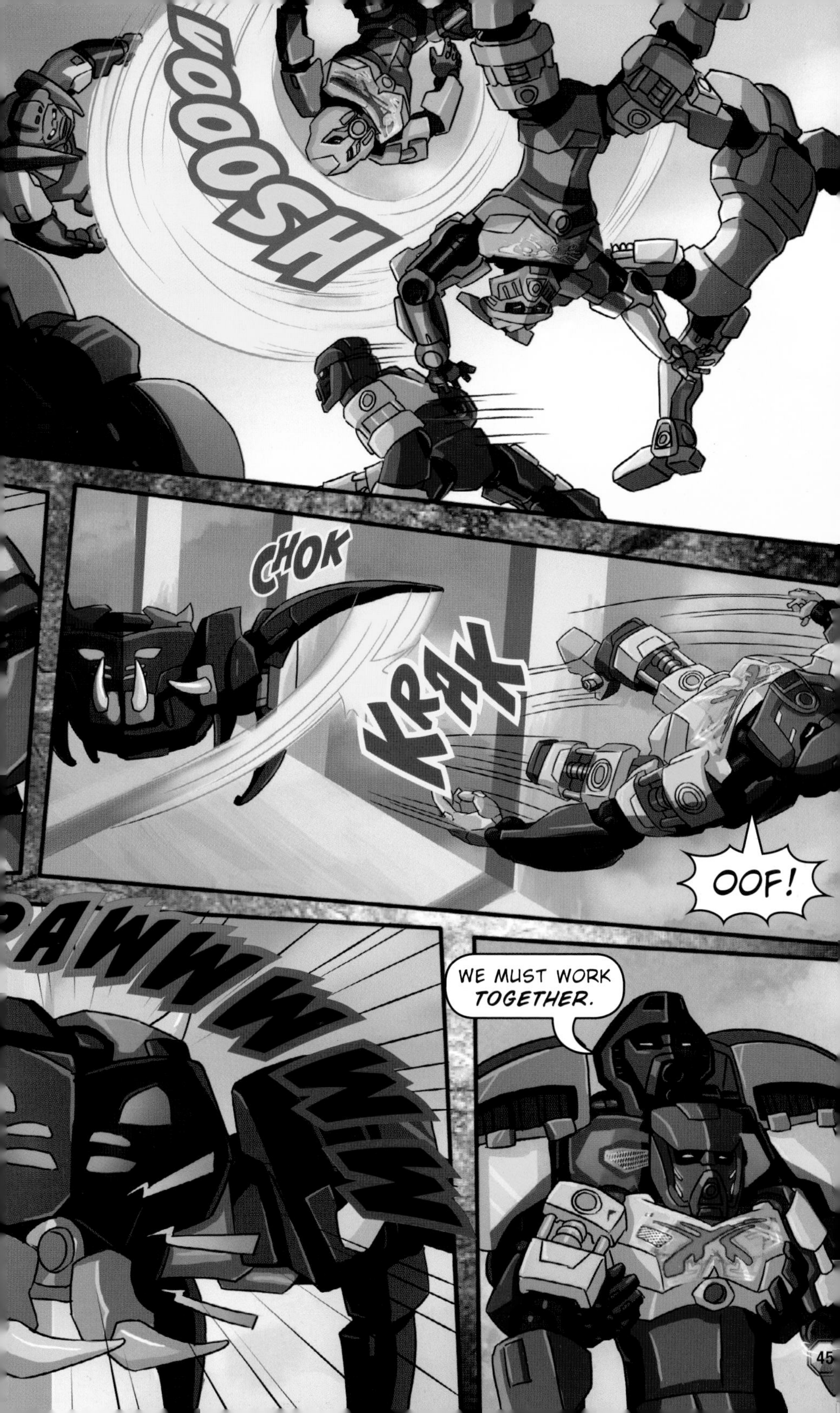
WOOOSH
CHOK
KRAK
OOF!
WE MUST WORK *TOGETHER.*

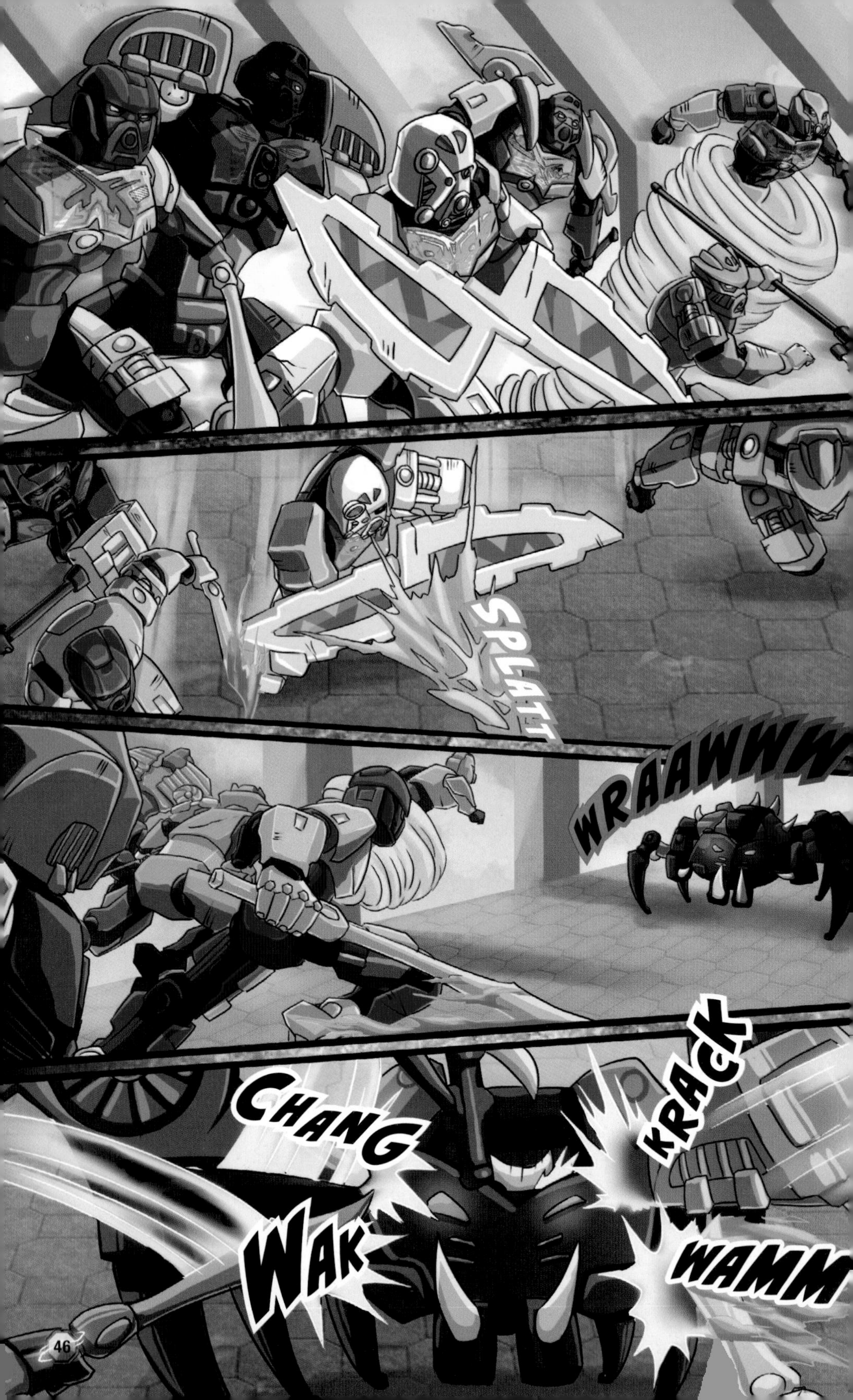
SPLATT
WRAAWWW
CHANG
KRACK
WAK
WAMM

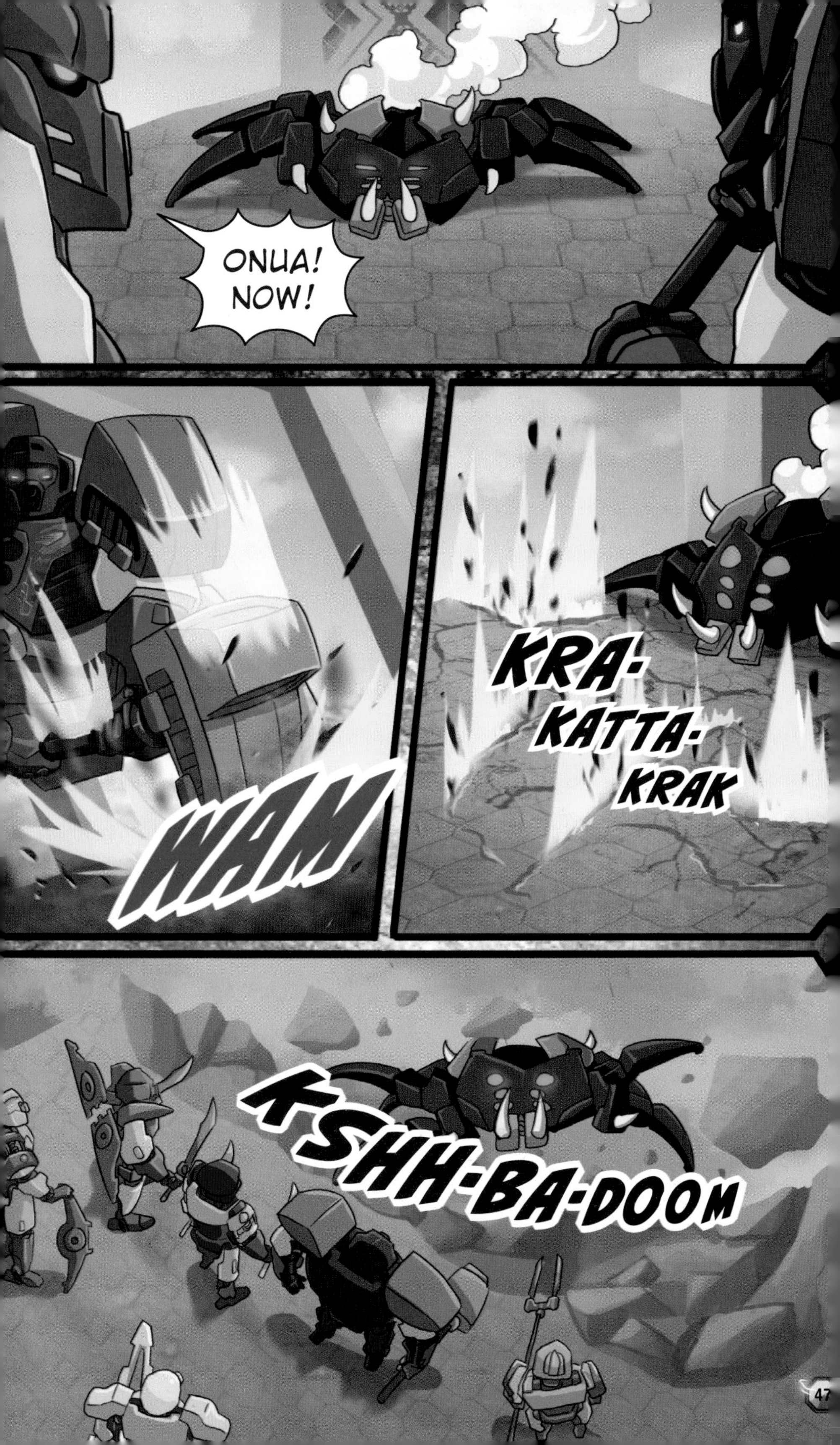
ONUA! NOW!
WAM
KRA-KATTA-KRAK
KSHH-BA-DOOM

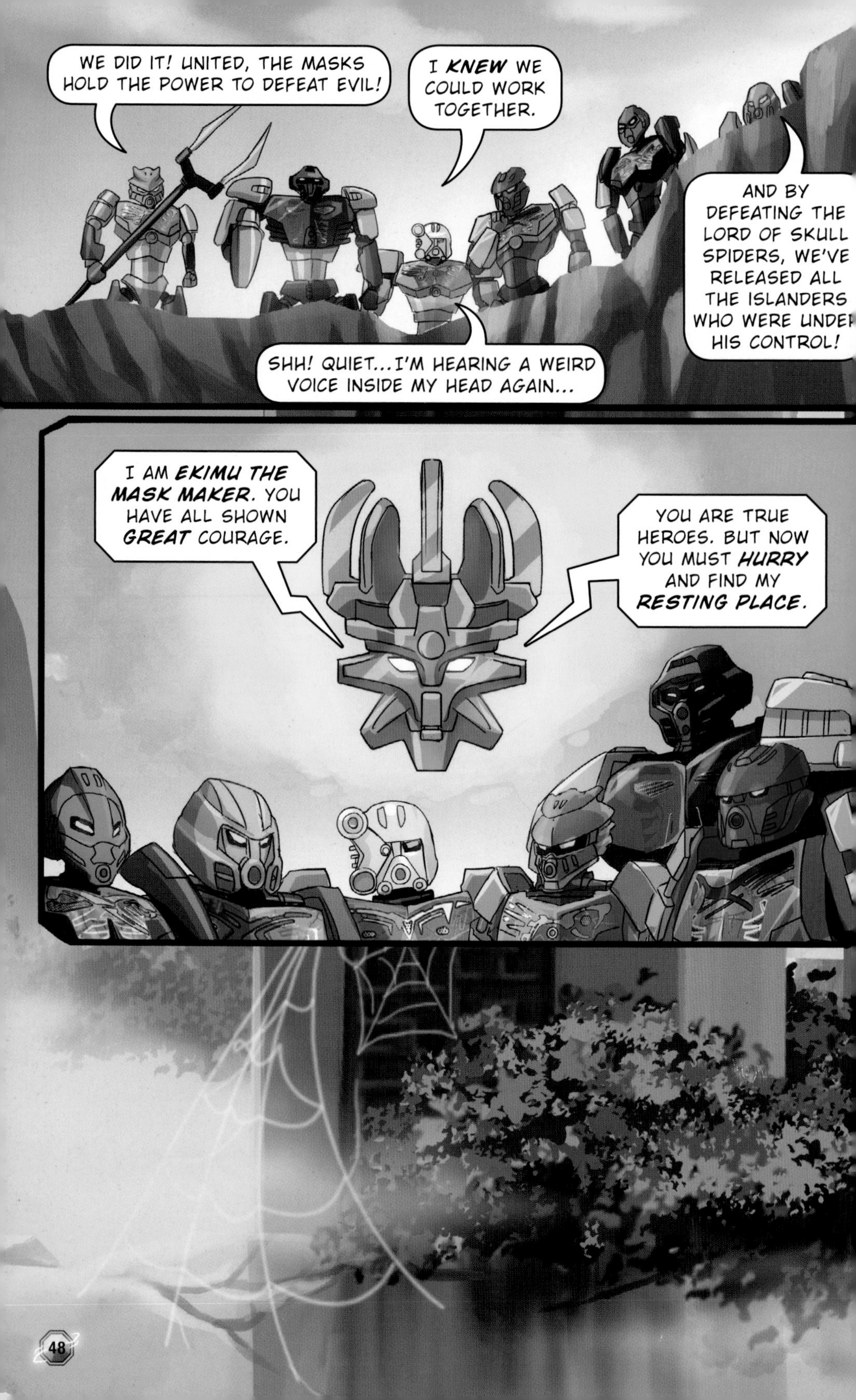
WE DID IT! UNITED, THE MASKS HOLD THE POWER TO DEFEAT EVIL!
I KNEW WE COULD WORK TOGETHER.
AND BY DEFEATING THE LORD OF SKULL SPIDERS, WE'VE RELEASED ALL THE ISLANDERS WHO WERE UNDER HIS CONTROL!
SHH! QUIET...I'M HEARING A WEIRD VOICE INSIDE MY HEAD AGAIN...
I AM EKIMU THE MASK MAKER. YOU HAVE ALL SHOWN GREAT COURAGE.
YOU ARE TRUE HEROES. BUT NOW YOU MUST HURRY AND FIND MY RESTING PLACE.

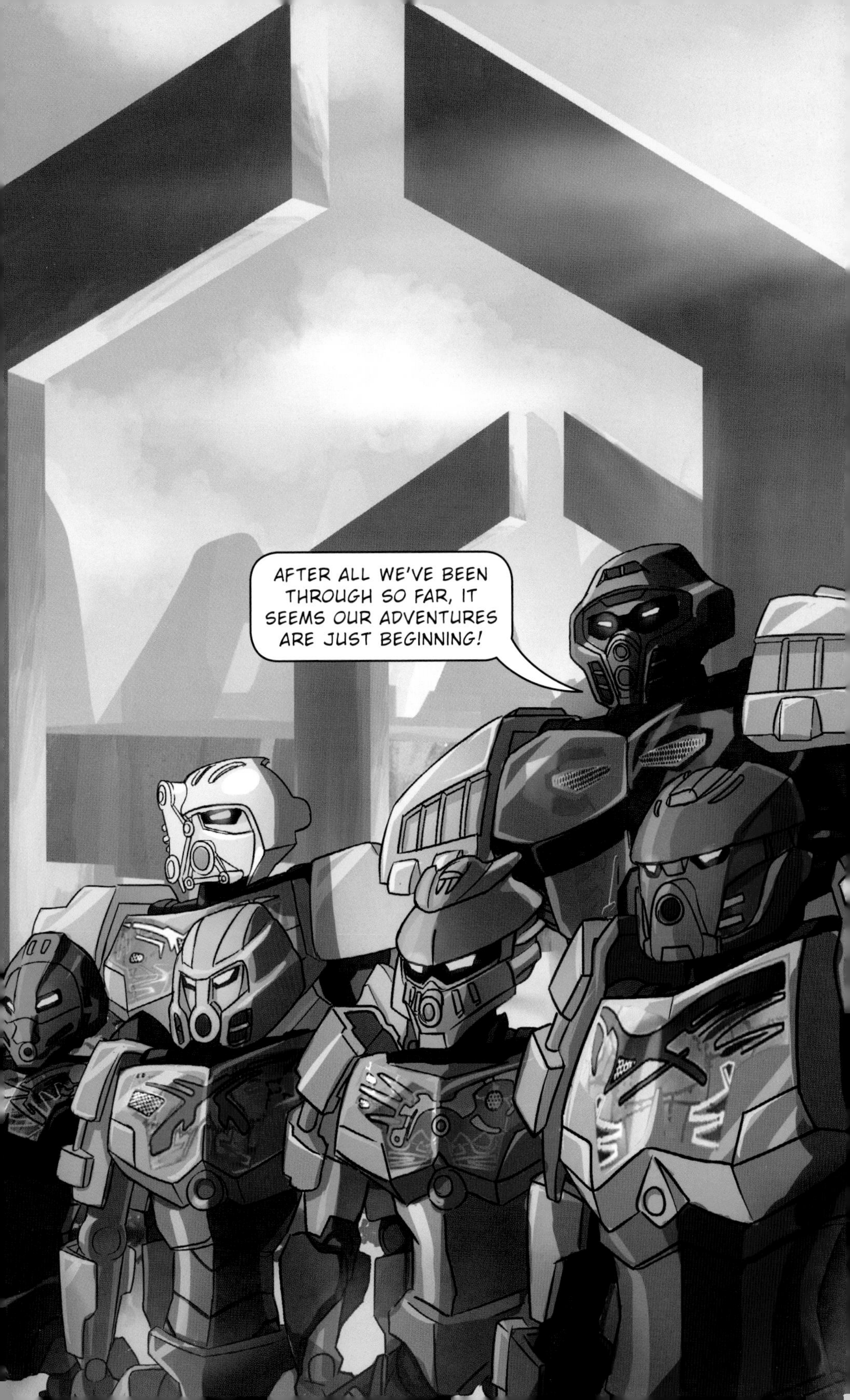
AFTER ALL WE'VE BEEN THROUGH SO FAR, IT SEEMS OUR ADVENTURES ARE JUST BEGINNING!

THE OKOTO
PROTECTORS GUIDE

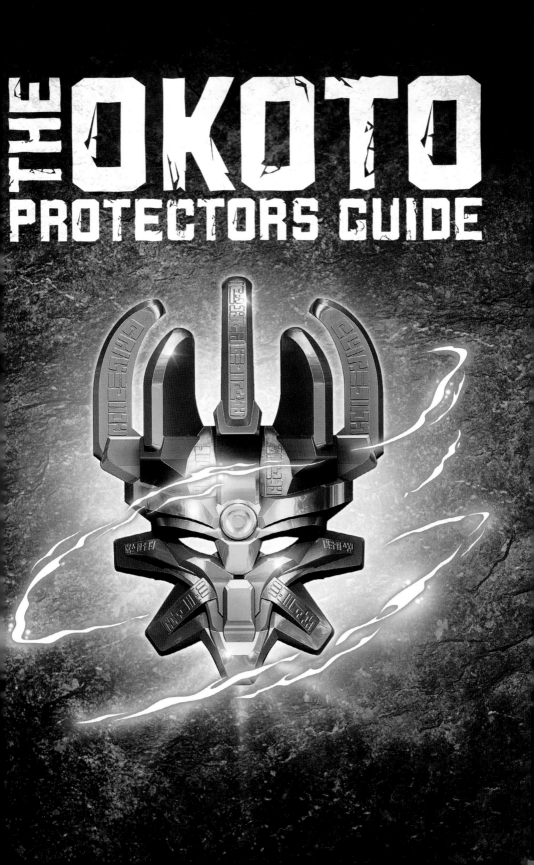

THE PROTECTORS GUIDE

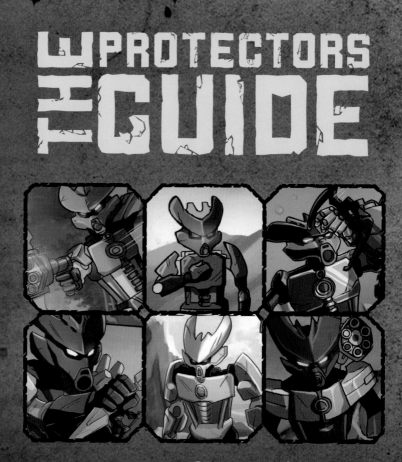

Many generations of Protectors have served as the peacekeepers and caretakers of the island of Okoto. Gathered around campfires, the Protectors recited the Prophecy of Heroes, which was first whispered to their ancestors by the sleeping body of Ekimu the Mask Maker after a devastating and historic battle with his evil brother, Makuta.

When times are dark and
all hope seems lost,
The Protectors must unite,
One from each tribe,
Evoke the power of past and future
And look to the skies for an answer.
When the stars align,
Six comets will bring timeless heroes
To claim the masks of power
And find the Mask Maker.
United, the elements hold
the power to defeat evil.
United but not one.

THE MASK MAKERS

Thousands of years ago, the brothers Ekimu and Makuta, known as the Mask Makers, used the elemental forces of the island of Okoto to create masks of power for the islanders. The islanders used their masks of power to shape their island, transforming it into a fantastic place full of wonders and beautiful landscapes.

The Mask Makers possessed special masks. Ekimu had the Mask of Creation, and Makuta had the Mask of Control. Although the brothers produced many masks, the islanders especially treasured the mask made by Ekimu. Makuta became envious of his brother's popularity, and came up with a treacherous plan to create the most powerful mask ever.

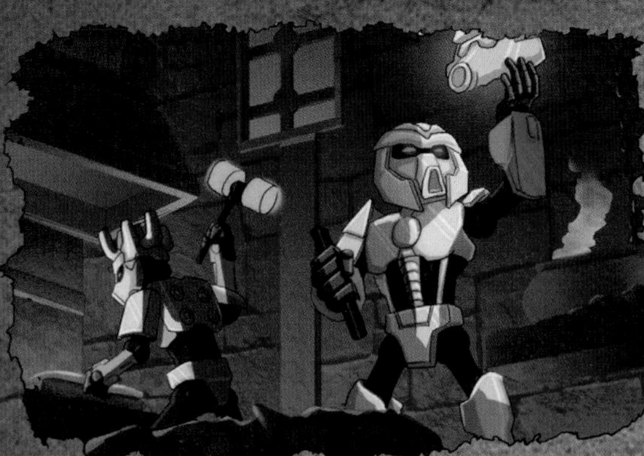

BATTLE FOR POWER

Although the Mask Makers knew that masks with more than one elemental power were extremely dangerous and difficult to control, Makuta channeled the island's six elements into a single mask, which he called the Mask of Ultimate Power. When Makuta put the mask on, its power overwhelmed him, and the island began to shake and crumble.

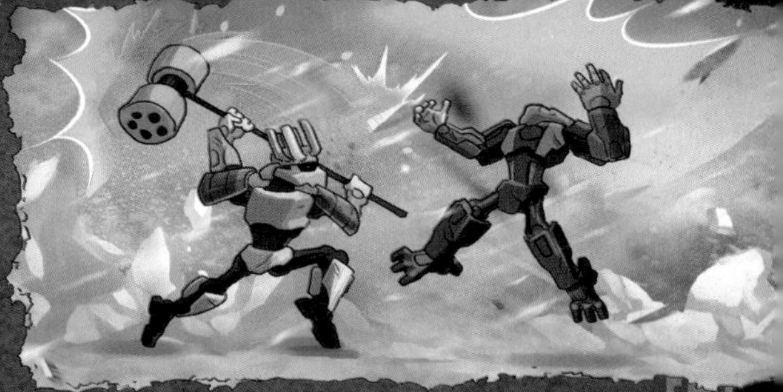

Realizing what Makuta had done, Ekimu managed to knock the mask off Makuta's face. The sudden disconnection caused a cataclysmic explosion that not only radically altered the island's geography—it also sent both brothers into a sleep that would last for millennia. The explosion also left many masks—including the brothers' masks and the Mask of Ultimate Power—scattered across the island.

MAP OF OKOTO

Once a paradise full of great forests and brimming with life, the island of Okoto was forever changed by the explosion of the Mask of Ultimate Power during the battle of the Mask Makers. The tremendous energy unleashed by the explosion destroyed the island's great cities and transformed Okoto into an island with six distinct regions, characterized by ice, water, jungle, fire, earth, and stone. Only the southern jungles, protected from the blast by the lee of the mountains, escaped the cataclysm.

THE GREAT CRATER

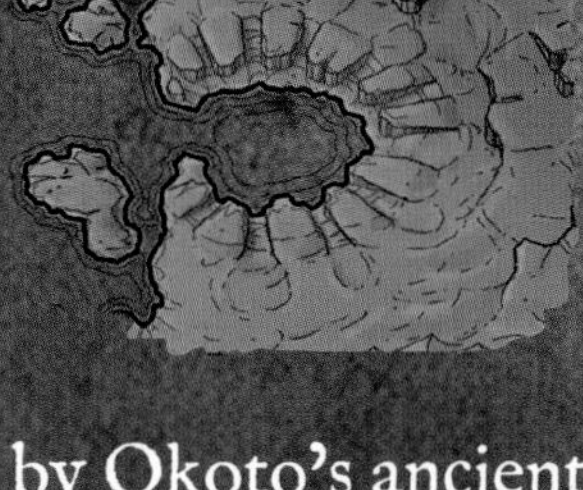

Once the site of a great capital built by Okoto's ancient civilization, and also the site of the battle of the Mask Makers, the Great Crater was formed by the explosion caused by the Mask of Ultimate Power.

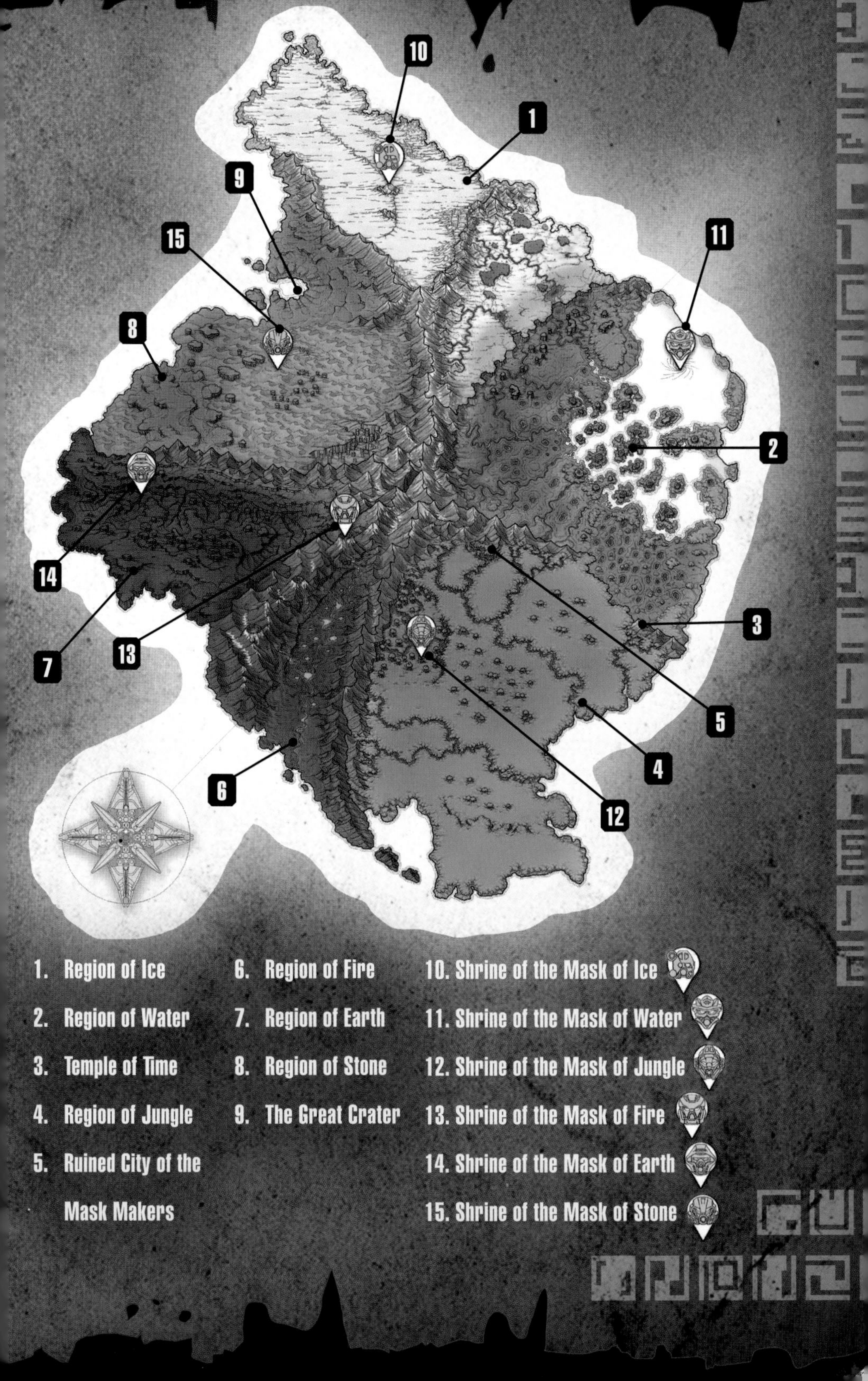

10
1
9
15
11
8
2
14
13
7
3
5
4
6
12

1. Region of Ice
2. Region of Water
3. Temple of Time
4. Region of Jungle
5. Ruined City of the Mask Makers
6. Region of Fire
7. Region of Earth
8. Region of Stone
9. The Great Crater
10. Shrine of the Mask of Ice
11. Shrine of the Mask of Water
12. Shrine of the Mask of Jungle
13. Shrine of the Mask of Fire
14. Shrine of the Mask of Earth
15. Shrine of the Mask of Stone

THE TEMPLE OF TIME

Perched on the peak of a small mountain on the eastern side of Okoto, between the Region of Water and the Region of Jungle, the Temple of Time is the Protectors' most sacred place. The Protectors believe the Temple of Time is the oldest structure on the entire island, and it is among the few structures that escaped destruction during the battle of the Mask Makers. The Protectors also believe

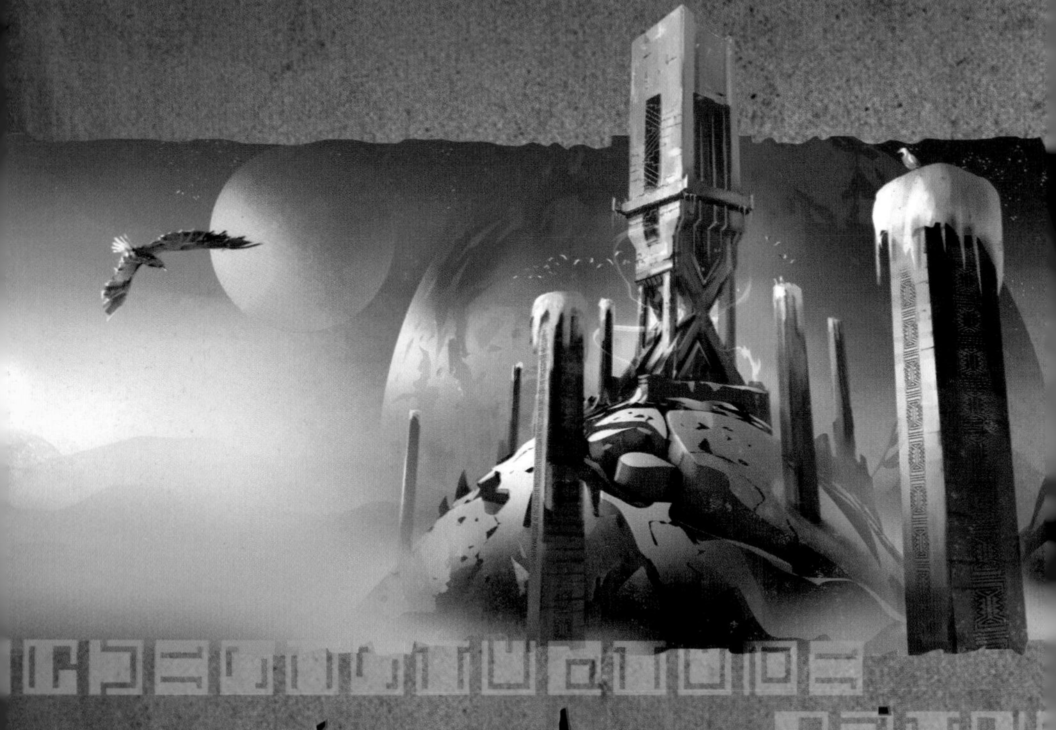

that the temple mystically connects Okoto with other places, including distant worlds, across time and space. When the Protectors finally realize that their own powers are not sufficient to stop the rising evil on Okoto, they go to the Temple of Time to recite the Prophecy of Heroes and summon the Toa.

THE MASK OF TIME

Kept in a secret vault in the Temple of Time, the Mask of Time possesses powers that even the wisest elders don't completely understand. According to ancient legends, the Mask of Time is actually a fragment of a larger mask: It is the upper half that completes the true Mask of Time.

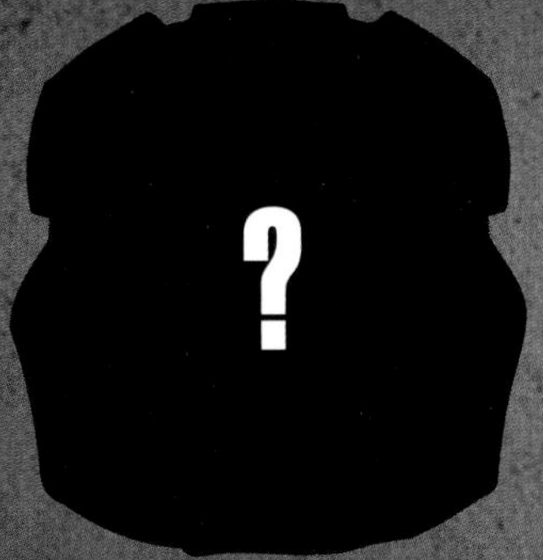
?

The Protectors do not possess any records or illustrations regarding the lower half of the Mask of Time and are unaware of its location.

THE PROTECTORS

Six Protectors, one from each regional tribe on Okoto, are tasked with helping to guide the six Toa on their quests. The Protectors wear sacred Elemental Masks that have been passed down through many generations. Each carries uniquely personal weapons that were engineered for optimal use in their home regions. Because of their duties and the vastness of their island, the six Protectors rarely gather in the same location at the same time.

Protector of Ice

Name: Izotor

Weapons: Elemental ice blaster, ice saw

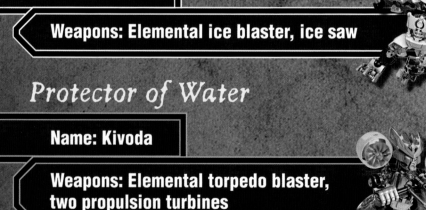

Protector of Water

Name: Kivoda

Weapons: Elemental torpedo blaster, two propulsion turbines

Protector of Jungle

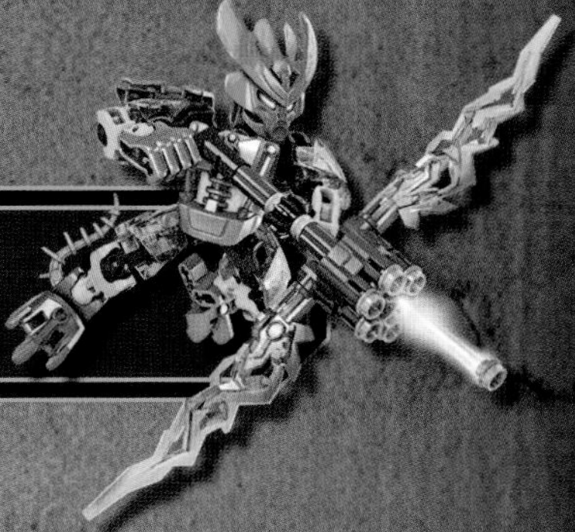

Name: Vizuna

Weapons: Air elemental flame bow, sensor tail

Protector of Fire

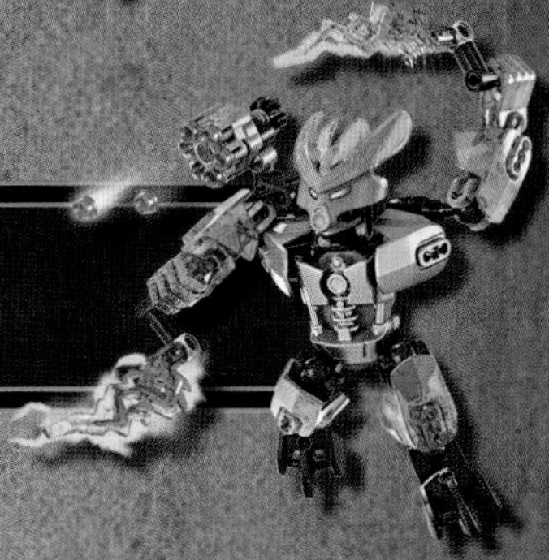

Name: Narmoto

Weapons: Elemental fire blaster, two flame swords

Protector of Earth

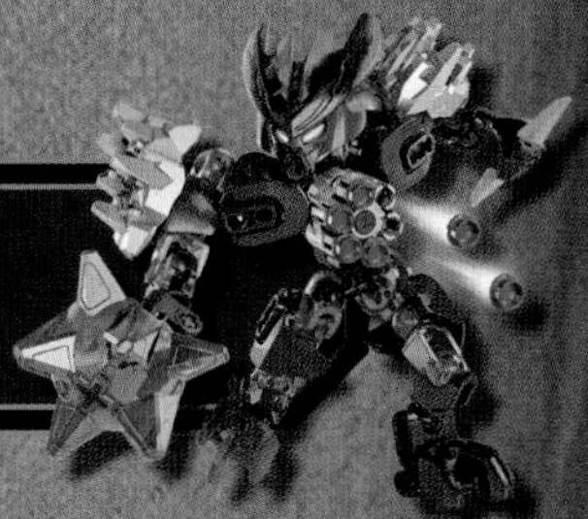

Name: Korgot

Weapons: Rapid shooter, two throwing knives, adamantine star drill

Protector of Stone

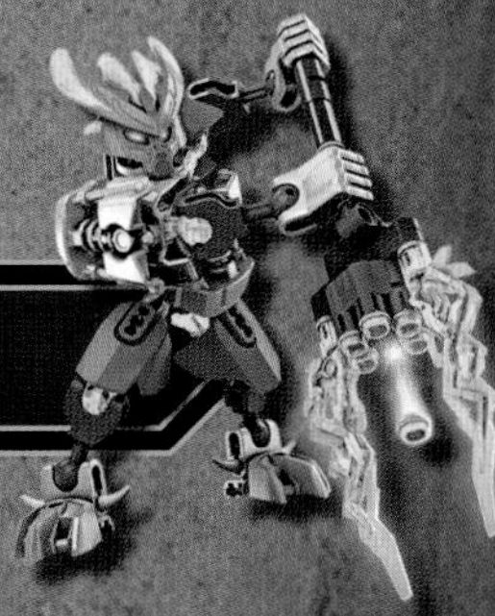

Name: Nilkuu

Weapon: Elemental sandstone blaster

THE HEROES

Delivered by comets to the island of Okoto, the six Toa are timeless heroes who respectively represent the island's six elemental forces: ice, water, jungle, fire, earth, and stone. Where they came from or who sent them remains a mystery, but their arrival was anticipated by the ancient Prophecy of Heroes, which foretold that they would come and save Okoto in a time of darkness.

Master of Ice

Name: Kopaka

Weapons: Ice spear, frost shield, avalanche skis

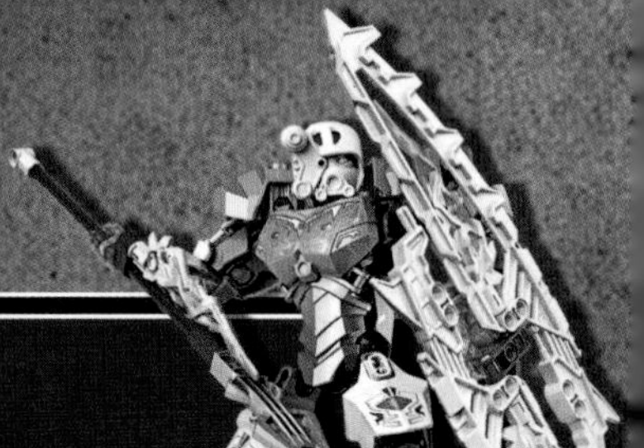

Master of Water

Name: Gali

Weapons: Harpoon, elemental trident, shark fins

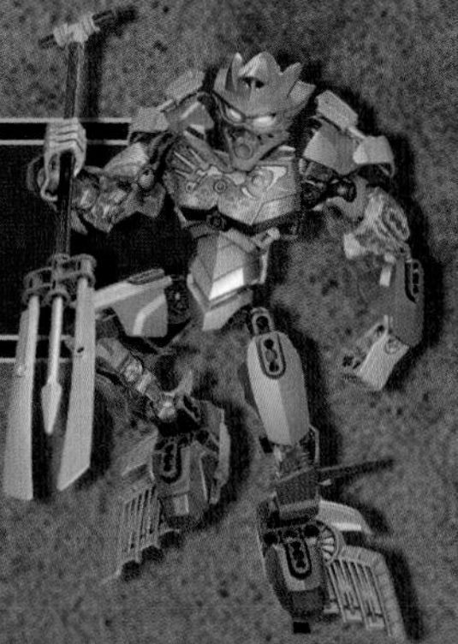

Master of Jungle

Name: Lewa

Weapons: Two battle axes, two swords, X-glider

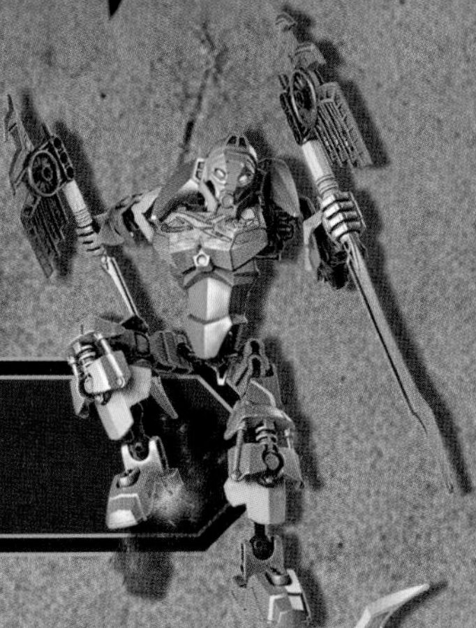

Master of Fire

Name: Tahu

Weapons: Fire blades, two golden swords

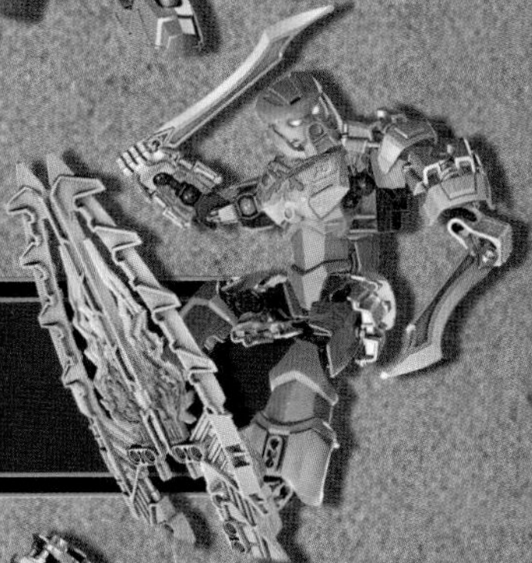

Master of Earth

Name: Onua

Weapons: Earthquake hammer, turbo shovelers

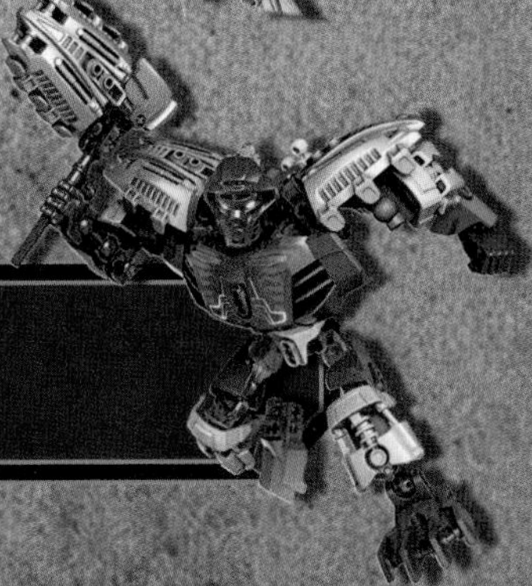

Master of Stone

Name: Pohatu

Weapons: Dagger, two stormerangs

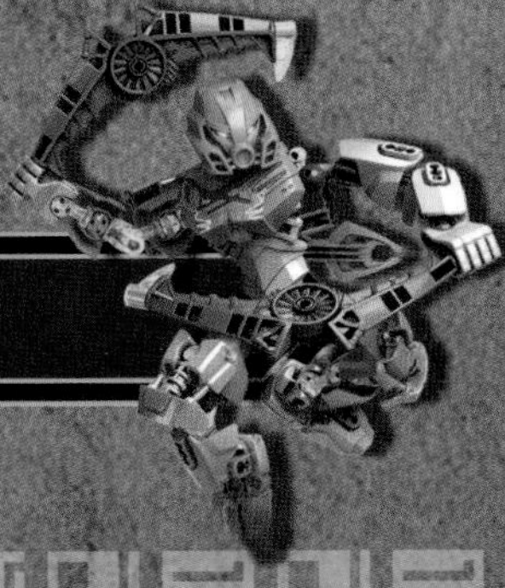

LORD OF SKULL SPIDERS

An evil-eyed, six-legged creature, the monstrous Lord of Skull Spiders patrols and guards the bridge to the ancient City of the Mask Makers. As his name implies, the Lord of Skull Spiders controls all the Skull Spiders, using a telepathic link to make them locate and steal every mask they can find. The Lord of Skull Spiders spits sticky webbing at his enemies and is also the master of a powerful death-lock attack that can squeeze the air out of even the toughest hero.

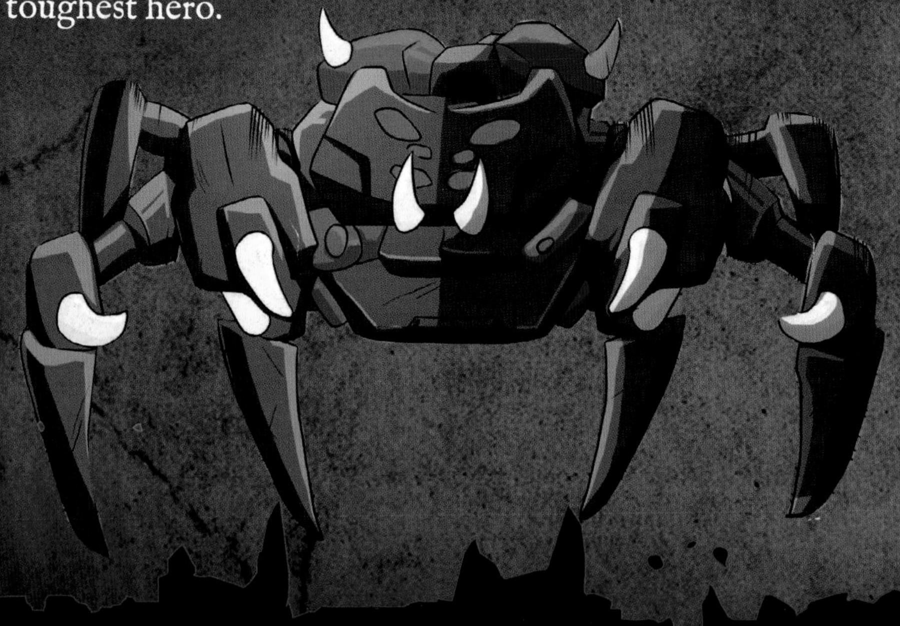

Solve This Code

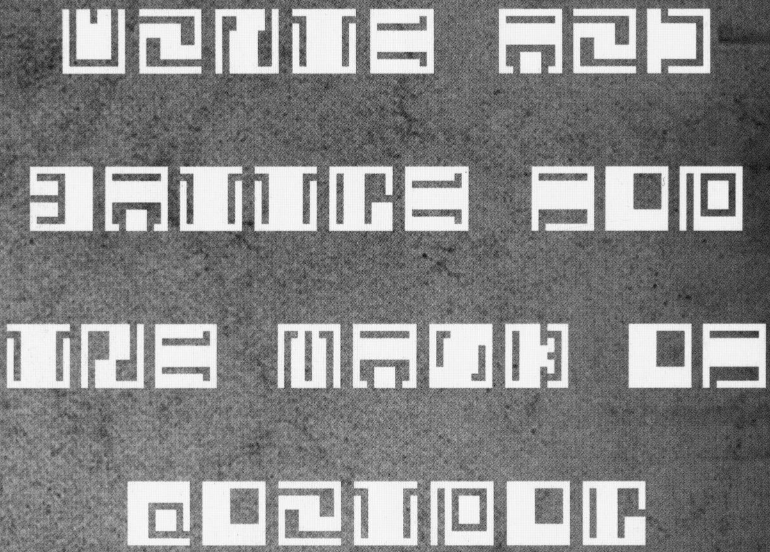

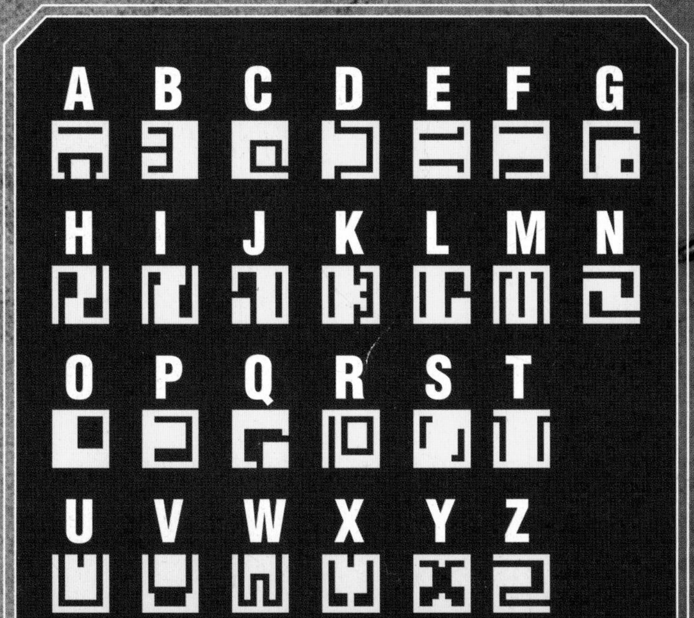
A B C D E F G
H I J K L M N
O P Q R S T
U V W X Y Z

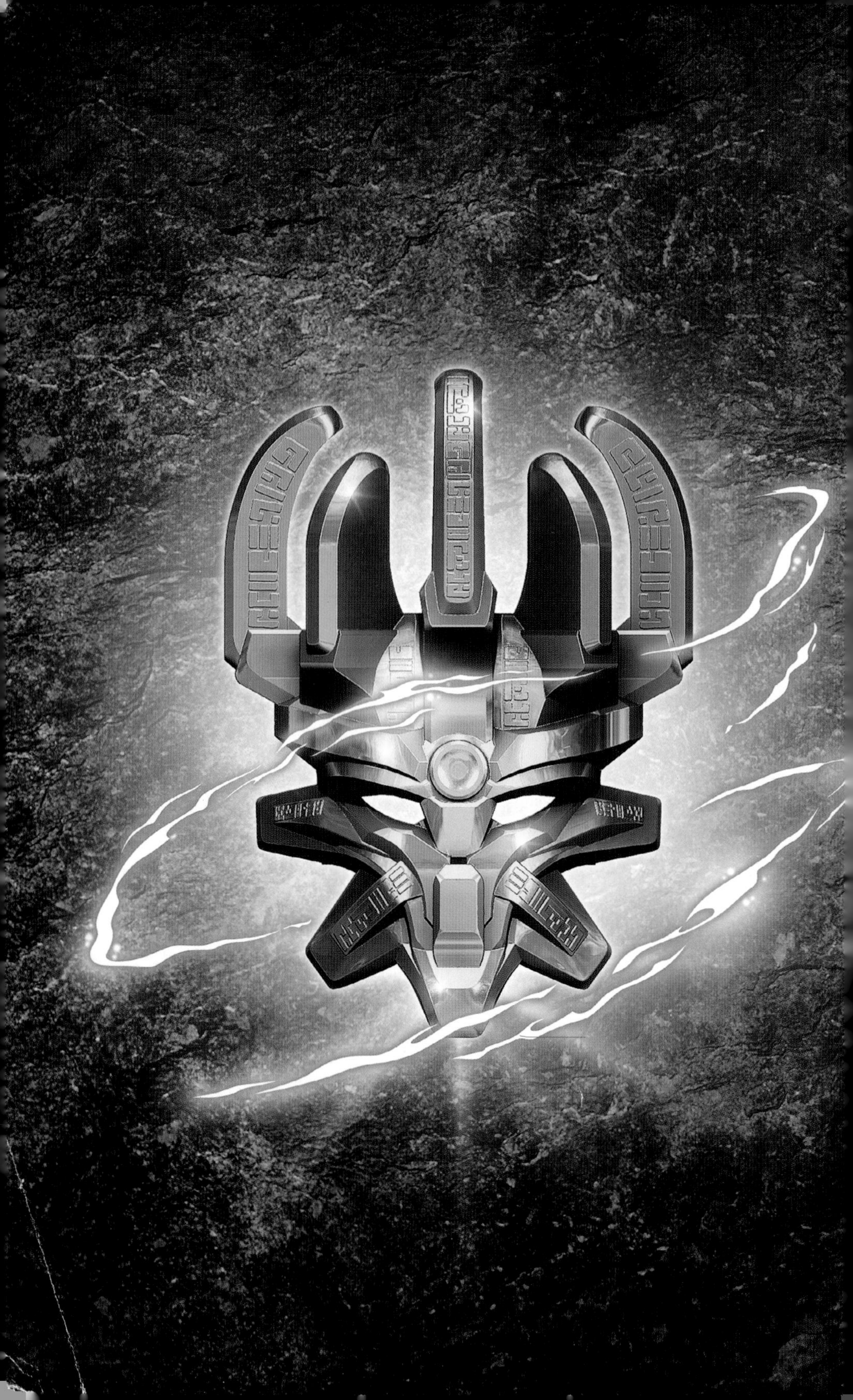